TEACH ME THE ROPES

BACHELOR AUCTION - BOOK 1

VANESSA VALE

Teach Me The Ropes by Vanessa Vale

Copyright © 2021 by Bridger Media

This is a work of fiction. Names, characters, places and incidents are the products of the author's imagination and used fictitiously. Any resemblance to actual persons, living or dead, businesses, companies, events or locales is entirely coincidental.

All rights reserved.

No part of this book may be reproduced in any form or by any electronic or mechanical means, including information storage and retrieval systems, without written permission from both authors, except for the use of brief quotations in a book review.

Cover design: Bridger Media

Cover graphic: Wander Aguiar Photography; Deposit Photos: design west

1

 ELSEY

"THINK HE'S BIG *EVERYWHERE*?"

"I bet it's as big as his bank balance. God, could you imagine taking a rich dick for a ride? I bet he likes it a little rough. Yeah, I'd cheat with him."

I held the preschool door open for Tanner to run back outside to the playground. He'd gotten mud all over his hands, and I'd taken him to get washed up. As he dashed off to the slide, I overheard the two moms chatting.

"Mmm, I wouldn't mind being pressed up against a

wall by him. I'm going to find a way to make that happen."

It was afternoon pickup time, and the women had arrived a few minutes earlier. They were sitting together on one of the benches within the fenced playground area. While their voices were tipped low because the subject wasn't for little ears, I couldn't miss their words. Or the direction they were staring. Or who they were staring at.

A man. A big, hot, cowboy in the parking lot.

He closed the driver's door on an old pickup truck—that definitely hid the size of his bank balance—set his Stetson on his head and made his way over to the low fence, his gait long. I didn't miss the play of muscles beneath his well-worn jeans or the way the sleeves of his white button-up were rolled up and showed off corded forearms. He leaned down and set his hands on the tops of the rails and smiled as he watched the kids.

Whoa. That smile was lethal. For my panties.

I'd never seen him before, but that didn't mean anything. I'd only worked at the preschool for a few months, and since it was summer, kids came on random days based on vacation plans.

Claire, a five-year old with her blonde hair in a

single braid down her back, ran over to him and flung her arms up.

Her father easily tossed her up in the air and gave her a noisy kiss on her cheek. She giggled then wiggled in his hold to get down. He set her back on her sneakered feet, and she ran off to the swings, not yet ready to leave because she'd just learned how to pump her legs and swing by herself.

My ovaries just exploded watching the two of them. There was nothing sweeter—and oddly arousing—than seeing a guy being so good with his child. It wasn't only me who felt that way since the two other women were fanning themselves with their hands as they continued to stare his way.

Those ladies? They already had kids. Men of their own. They could fantasize about Mr. Hot Cowboy all they wanted because they were going to go home and get some from their husbands.

Me? No husband. No boyfriend. The only getting some I'd get was from my vibrator.

I frowned, the hot cowboy thoughts knocked to the curb by the bitterness that thinking about my ex brought on. The asshole had been smooth and a two-timer. Sure, I'd gotten myself in my current mess all by myself by being gullible and too free with my feelings, but Tom had also lied out his ass telling me he was single. Only when I'd loaded up my car and followed him did I find out he was far, far from it. A wife and two kids didn't make a guy single, that was for fucking sure. Leaving my life in Colorado behind had been plain stupid, and now I was stuck here.

Of course, that wasn't *all* Tom's fault. After finding out about his secret family, I'd chosen a horrible roommate off the Internet who'd decided to steal all my belongings except my clothes... plus my rent money and left me high and dry. Broke and evicted. *That* was how I was stuck in Montana.

I shouldn't have trusted Tom. I shouldn't have trusted Laila, the klepto. I thought I'd learned from my mother and the way she clung to man after man, always being kicked to the curb after they were tired of her. Since she only contacted me after her latest breakup, I assumed she was still in Phoenix with guy number seven. Or was it eight? Guys weren't to be trusted. And yet, I had. Just once.

I sighed, kicking myself the most for being more like my mom than I thought.

The women giggled which broke me from my thoughts. While Montana wasn't known for dressing up, they were stylish in jeans, cute tops and wedge sandals. Their hair was artfully tousled, and their makeup subtle but effective. If the hot cowboy was going to go for a woman on the preschool playground, it was going to be one of them. Definitely not me in my old jeans and sneakers. My t-shirt had blue paint on the front, and my hair was pulled back out of my face in a simple ponytail although the slight breeze had tugged some wild curls free.

I had no idea why I was even thinking this guy would choose any one of us. No doubt he was married. *Of course,* he was married, especially since one of the women said it would be cheating. His wife probably had blonde hair like their daughter's and knew just how big he was. *Everywhere.*

"Mommy, Claire pulled my hair." The whiny voice came from Tamara, who was complaining to one of the moms. She'd just turned four and was cute as could be but was definitely going to be a handful as she got older.

Tamara's mother, who had the same dark hair but not in pigtails, lifted her head and scanned the playground. I did, too. Claire was still on the swings, laughing at something Tanner was saying as he sat on the swing beside hers.

The woman stood, took Tamara's hand and came over to me. "You need to punish Claire. She's mean."

I arched a brow but didn't say anything, only squatted down in front of Tamara. Guys I couldn't deal with, but kids? I had them down. Giving her a small smile, I said. "Hair pulling, huh?"

She nodded, her pigtails bobbing. "It hurt."

"I haven't seen you anywhere near Claire on the playground."

"She did it," Tamara countered right away, her lower lip sticking out.

I cocked my head. "I'm not saying she didn't, but when did she do it, honey?"

Tamara looked up at her mom.

"Does it matter?" the woman asked. "I believe my daughter. What are you going to do about it?"

"I am doing something about it," I replied, tipping my chin up, so I could meet the mom's eyes. "We talk out our problems here. When did Claire pull your hair?" My gaze flicked to Tamara.

She bit her lip and glanced at me then away. "Yesterday when we were taking off our jackets."

Even though it was summer, some mornings were cool. Like yesterday when I'd had to wear a sweatshirt until after lunch.

"Did you tell someone then about what happened?" I asked.

Tamara shook her head.

"There isn't a statute of limitations on bad behavior," Tamara's mom said. I couldn't miss the way she tapped her foot since I was close to the ground.

I ignored her and focused on Tamara. It was obvious where she was modeling her bad behavior, so I had to be a good example here. "What happened exactly?"

She put her finger to her neck as she spoke. "I was taking off my jacket, and my hair got caught in my zipper. Claire helped, but it pulled."

I stood up and patted Tamara on the head. "Sounds like you need to tell your jacket to stop being so mean. I hope you thanked Claire for helping."

Tamara looked at the ground then gave a sly glance at her mother. "No."

I didn't say anything, just let Tamara take a minute to figure out what she needed to do. "Thanks, Claire!" she called across the playground then tugged on her mom's hand. "I'm ready to go now."

Of course, she was since she hadn't gotten the attention from her mother she'd been seeking.

The mom eyed me up and down as if she was confused how I'd spun the situation around, getting a zipper to be the bad guy. Without saying anything further, the duo cut across the playground to the side gate that led to the parking lot.

I sighed, watching them go, wondering how the

woman could walk in those high heels. I'd never be that girly-girl.

"Thank you."

The voice came from behind me, and I spun about and practically ran into Mr. Hot Cowboy. My hand flew to my chest. "Fudge, you scared me."

"Easy there." He cupped my elbow as if to settle me.

All of a sudden, it was *very* warm out and not from the afternoon sun. My heart skipped a beat as I stared up, up, up at Claire's father. I'd totally missed him leaving his spot by the fence. He must have gone inside while I'd been talking to Tamara and her mom because he held Claire's little pink backpack.

This close, I couldn't miss that his eyes were fair even though his hair was dark. The contrast was striking. So was the chiseled jaw with dark scruff, as if he hadn't shaved in a few days. He stared down at me, his gaze raking over my face, my body, then back to my... lips?

"Fudge?" he asked, the corner of his mouth tipped up.

I frowned, glancing at his hand. Instantly, he pulled it away.

"Job requirement," I replied. "Gotta filter those f-bombs."

He was looking at me. Studying me even, his eyes looking between mine then sweeping down to my mouth then back. "I overheard your little chat with Tamara. She's just like her momma and is starting to twist things around to her advantage. I've known Delilah since we were kids, and she hasn't changed a bit."

I had a momma who liked to twist things around, too, but I wasn't telling him that. I couldn't stand his scrutiny and shifted my eyes to the button on his shirt. I felt my cheeks go hot. Damned fair skin.

"Well, yes." Talking bad about a four-year old—or her mother—wasn't the best idea.

I couldn't lose my job.

When I didn't say more, he added, "It's amazing one so young could be so skilled at it."

He wasn't wrong. I was glad I taught preschoolers and not teenagers because Tamara was going to raise hell in about ten years, I was sure of it.

I didn't say anything, only glanced at the kids who'd yet been picked up. The other preschool teacher, Sarah Jane, was on the far side of the playground keeping watch, talking to Tanner and moving her arms up and down, probably explaining how to pump his legs like Claire.

"I've been avoiding Delilah for years. I appreciate you having Claire's back."

I looked up at him then. His eyes wandered over my face again.

"Claire's a good girl," I shared.

"Are you?" he asked. Or that was what I thought he'd asked.

I frowned, I lifted my hand to my forehead to shield my eyes from the sun as I looked up at him. Had I heard him right? "Excuse me?"

He gripped my shoulders and turned me, so I wasn't blinded. Then he cleared his throat as he dropped his hands away. "I've never seen you here before. Are you new?" His voice was deep and rumbly.

When I took a deep breath to answer, I picked up his scent. Pine and woods and strong male.

"Yes. I've been in town about two months."

He offered an absent nod. "I'd have remembered you. God, that hair."

I touched my hand to my head. Blushed. I had wild red curls, and they were pulled back with a tie at my nape. Nothing tamed them no matter how hard I tried. Since I only had the hand dryers in the women's room at the community center to dry it, it was worse than ever.

He reached out, tugged on a tendril that had

escaped and stared at it as if mesmerized. I'd been picked on for red hair growing up, and I wasn't sure if he was poking fun or pleased.

"It's red," I said.

He grinned, met my eyes. "It sure as fuck is."

It's red? Seriously? That's what came out of my mouth? I glanced away, feeling like a complete idiot.

He dropped his hand and tucked it into the front pocket of his jeans.

"Where'd you come from?"

"Colorado, but I moved to The Bend for the job."

I wasn't going to elaborate any more than that. He didn't need to know about Tom or the shitty klepto roommate or the fact that I was broke. And pretty much homeless.

"I'm Sawyer Manning."

He held out his hand. I stared at it for a second then shook it. The zing I felt had me whipping my head up to meet his gaze. His grip was warm and firm, and I could feel callouses against my palm. I had no idea what he did to make all the money Delilah mentioned, but he didn't sit behind a desk.

"Kelsey."

"Anyone ever told you you're beautiful?"

His voice was soft, and the words took a second to sink in.

Was he... was he flirting with me?

"Anyone tell you you're too forward?"

I tugged my hand, trying to get it back from the handshake, but he wouldn't let go. He grinned.

"Um, I—"

Tanner's mom arrived, and she waved to me as the little boy ran to her at the gate. I tugged once more, and he released my hand. I waved back to both of them before they left, but my thoughts were on the very big, very sexy guy beside me.

"Since you're new, why don't I show you around town," he said.

I blinked at him then came out of my hot guy induced stupor. Just because he was cowboy calendar gorgeous didn't mean he wasn't a jerk. I'd been burned once before. I wasn't having that happen again. The Bend was small. *Really* small. If he knew Tamara's mom since they were kids, that meant he was from here. Knew everyone. I wasn't going to be *the other woman*. My mother might not have cared about a guy's relationship status before she shacked up with him, but I did.

Besides, if I lost my job at the preschool, I had no idea what I would do. I was sleeping in the building's back room. A short-term arrangement. The preschool's owner, Irene, had offered for me to stay at her house when she'd learned about my situation, but after one night with three elementary school kids—one who'd put peanut butter on my nose when I was sleeping—plus two dogs and a blind parakeet, I'd asked if I could make use of the small cot until I had the money I needed for an apartment deposit. She'd wanted to do more for me, but I wasn't going to inconvenience her or be beholden. I didn't have money, but I had my pride. The way I was saving, I hoped to be in an apartment in a few more weeks.

I'd been stupid before, and that was on me. But no longer. I stepped away from Sawyer Manning and shook my head. I'd done nothing wrong. I had my eyes wide open this time. *He* was the asshole. God, he was a total player! Picking up women on the playground while his daughter was on the swing? I couldn't decide if Tom had been worse keeping his family a secret and stringing me along or this guy, blatantly asking me out while I fully knew he had a child. A wife. At least he wasn't a liar. But still...

I could only imagine what he thought of me. A slut? Worse, a home wrecker? Had he worked his way through all the women in town who knew him?

Crossing my arms over my chest, I tipped up my chin. Met his gaze. "No."

"No?" he asked, his eyebrows going up and disappearing beneath his hat, seemingly shocked at my answer. "You sure because I grew up here and know all the secret spots."

If he weren't married, I'd love for him to show me all the *secret spots*. On my body. But since he was, his words only pissed me off even more.

"I said no," I replied then glanced around to ensure no kids were nearby. "If you need me to be more clear, how's this? No. Fudging. Way."

Turning away from him, I caught Sarah Jane's attention and gave her the signal that it was time for me to leave for the day. Since I was crashing in the preschool's back room at night, I opened in the morning and someone else closed. She nodded then gave me a little wave and I fled inside.

I was so keyed up I was shaky. Tom had done a number on me, but this guy? God, he had nerve. There was a big dick in his pants, but he had balls too. Really big ones.

How did I keep attracting assholes? What the fuck was wrong with me? I opened one of the high cabinets in the back room, the one the kids couldn't reach, and pulled down my purse.

A hand settled on my shoulder, and I shrieked.

"Look, I'm sorry I—"

I processed the voice, the words, in the same

instant I just reacted. Maybe it was everything I'd been going through, maybe Sawyer Manning had been a trigger for all the shit I'd pushed down that had happened because of Tom. The fallout I was still living through now.

Or maybe he was just a dick.

I spun on my heel and kneed him in the balls. He bent at the waist, dropped to his knees, then tipped over onto his side in a fetal position on the industrial carpet. His hands cupped his crotch.

"Oh shit," I whispered as he groaned from the floor. I glanced at the door, hoped Sarah Jane didn't come in with any of the other kids, or Claire in search of her dad.

My breath came out in pants, my adrenaline pumping. I stared down at him, noticed the way his face had turned white and couldn't miss the wheezing coming from his lungs. I hadn't meant to knee one of the preschool's clients in the balls. I'd just acted without thinking. In anger.

This was bad. Really bad, even though he deserved it.

This was what I'd wanted to do to my ex. Hit him where it counted, but I never got the chance.

"I've had enough of guys like you," I said, setting my hands on my hips. He was clearly in misery.

Served him right. "Try your flirting shit on someone else."

Grabbing my bag and keys, I stormed out the front door. I'd taught Sawyer Manning a lesson, but had I learned one too? The hard way, like losing my job and where I slept at night?

2

SAWYER

"A BACHELOR AUCTION? You're shitting me," Huck said, running a hand over the back of his neck, staring wide eyed then dropped into the stool at the counter.

"Language," Alice scolded. She'd stopped chopping the carrots for the stew for dinner and gave him her familiar withering glare. Even though we were grown men, that didn't keep her from reminding the three of us of our manners.

My brother only grinned back, if a little sheepishly. It was the look that had gotten him out of messes growing up and still got women out of their panties.

Since he was the chief of police now, he'd grown out of being a hellion but not out of charming the ladies. "Fine. *You've got to be joking,*" he said instead.

A smile turned up the corner of our housekeeper's mouth as she looked from Huck to Thatcher to me. The three Manning brothers. *Bachelor* brothers to her disappointment. They were in the kitchen with Alice as she prepped dinner. I was on the couch in the great room—the open space that was part family room, dining room and connected to the kitchen—with a bag of frozen peas on my crotch.

As soon as we'd gotten back to the ranch, I unhooked Claire from her booster seat, and she'd run off toward the stable where Roy had promised her a pony ride. After I saw her meet up with the older ranch hand, I'd headed inside and right to the freezer. When I'd dropped onto the couch and put the package over my... package, Alice had arched a brow but hadn't said a word.

My annoying brothers had, and I'd had to give them a play-by-play. More like blow-by-blow. Fuck.

They'd thought I'd been joking at first, but the peas resting on my jeans-covered crotch had set them straight. They'd even winced and put their hands over their own junk in instinctual male protection. With a little distance and recovery time, I'd had to laugh because a woman had dropped me like fucking Redwood. Not many caught me by surprise, but Kelsey sure as shit had.

I knew what to watch out for next time. There *would* be a next time. No woman had intrigued me like she had in... ever, which meant I'd lost my mind. She was feisty, bad tempered and had it in for me.

I'd laid on the floor of the preschool for a few minutes after she'd stormed out. Partially because I'd been unable to move and partially because she'd destroyed my pride. I'd thought of our short conversation ever since and tried to figure out what I'd said or done that had pissed her off that much.

I didn't hurt women. I didn't fuck with them. String them along. I was the *nice* Manning brother. I sure as shit hadn't done anything to Kelsey, and yet she seemed to have a fucking hair trigger, and I'd somehow pulled it. I thought I'd behaved the gentleman in the few minutes we'd talked.

I'd offered to show her around town, not around my dick.

"I'm not joking," Alice repeated. "A bachelor auction Friday night, and all three of you are in it."

Thatcher glanced my way but didn't seem too bothered by the idea. He'd come in from the stables and sported jeans, held up by a belt and the Junior

Steer Roping champ belt buckle, and t-shirt. His t-shirt was as dusty as his sturdy work boots. There was a crease in his red hair from his Stetson, which hung on a hook by the back door next to mine. He worked as bartender at the Lucky Spur downtown, but that was at night. During the day, he pretty much ran the ranch.

Huck gave me a grim look, as if he were heading to the gallows on Friday instead of a fundraiser. He shifted uncomfortably, adjusting his utility belt, heavy with radio, cuffs, holster and pistol. Between the two of us, we had the chief roles down. He was the chief of police for The Bend. I was the fire chief. I'd had the day off, so I'd volunteered to pick up Claire, so Alice hadn't had to go back into town.

I shifted the ice cold peas in my lap, remembering what that kindness had gotten me.

"I admit," she said with a small shrug of her shoulder, "I will get some amusement from watching you three squirm up there on stage."

"At our expense," I called, adjusting the pillow behind my head.

She set those gray eyes on me. "A woman's paying the tab. No expense to you." The corner of her mouth twitched, and she was intentionally being sassy. As if the older woman was *ever* sassy.

"It's for a good cause," she added, reminding me we couldn't complain. But that didn't stop Huck.

"Yeah, but here? The Bend is so small, who's going to bid?" he asked.

Huck and I were public servants. We were used to helping the community. Hell, we put our lives on the line every time we took a shift. But this was definitely a new twist.

Thatcher went around the kitchen island and snagged a carrot chunk from the board and popped it in his mouth. Alice slapped his hand but gave him an indulgent look. "If I'm going to be forced on a date with the highest bidder, I don't want it to be Miss Turnbuckle from the library," he advised. "I want to use my time *wisely*."

I had a feeling *wisely* meant in bed with his head between a woman's legs as she screamed his name, but I wasn't going to say that. Not in front of Alice.

I'd like to use my time *wisely* with the gorgeous redhead who'd shot me down. I'd gone down in flames, hard core.

No. Fudging. Way, she'd said.

With those words, she'd made it pretty damned clear she wanted nothing to do with me. I'd watched her walk inside, and I'd stood on the playground, stunned. It wasn't as if I'd asked her to hop in my bed.

I hadn't told her what I'd been thinking, about how I wanted to bend her over the side of my bed and fuck her hard, to find out if a good girl like her liked to get her ass spanked. Or how those plump lips looked spread wide around my dick. Any of those would have deserved a knee to the balls.

But I hadn't said any of that, and she'd practically ripped me a new one. Any sane guy would have gotten the message and headed in the opposite direction, but I'd gone inside to apologize and make it right, which had gone so fucking wrong.

"I'm sure Selma Turnbuckle will be there and might just bid on one of you and win. If she does, you will be a proper gentleman," she warned, waving her knife in each of our directions. The woman was the ranch's housekeeper and all-around mother hen. And she wanted us married.

That was all fine and good, but I didn't want to be sold to the highest bidder. I wasn't fucking a cow. I'd sure feel like a piece of meat up on the community center's stage as women bid on what they saw; me and my brothers and the other men who'd been wrangled into participating.

Part of going on a date was the hope of *not* being a proper gentleman at the end of it. But Miss Turnbuckle, the town librarian, had to be seventy if she was a day. She had gray hair when I was a kid. I had nothing but gentlemanly thoughts where she was concerned. Maybe she wouldn't be a bad date. She always loved that Momma had named us after Mark Twain characters. I'd escort her home and be done.

It had been a long time since I'd felt any kind of real attraction to a woman. Years. Until earlier. Until Kelsey. The first time I'd seen her across the playground I'd felt like a cartoon character with my eyes popping out of my head and my dick instantly hard. She was just that fucking pretty. I was thirty-fucking-four years old and was far from a monk but had never once felt this way. Like being hit by a fence rail upside the head.

I wanted the whole deal. The heated looks, the flirting, the foreplay, the sweaty sex. Instead, I'd gotten a knee to the crotch. I must be insane because I still wanted Kelsey. Maybe more so because she'd stood up to me. For what, I didn't know. But I'd find out.

I should have my head examined because females were crazy. I'd had a woman who I'd thought was the real deal, but that had turned to shit. Tina. Thinking her name had the same effect on my dick as thinking of Miss Turnbuckle. I shifted the peas, winced.

"You said you want us happily wed," Thatcher said, snatching another carrot chunk.

He might be the youngest, but he was the biggest pain in the ass.

"Alice, a date with one of your friends isn't going to get us to the altar," he added.

She set her knife down and sighed. Wiped her hands on her apron. "I want you each to find a good woman." Her gaze shifted to mine when she said that, the importance on the word *good* because we all knew I'd found a woman—Tina—and that had been *bad.* "Make some babies."

I'd had no expectation of ever finding a *good* woman. Turned out, Tina had wanted the Manning land and the money that went with it more than me. When the pre-nup I'd presented her had brought out where her true interests had been, she'd left me. And the area.

No way could she fuck the town's fire chief then fuck him over and stay around. The Bend was too small for shit like that to fly. The chances of finding The One in rural Montana, who'd make me smile and make me come hard were fucking slim to none. I instantly thought of Kelsey. She'd made me smile. And she'd make me come so fucking hard—as soon as my balls recovered.

As for making babies, I was up at least to practice. A lot. I didn't even need a bed. I'd be all over practicing with Kelsey bent over my desk or in the back stall of the stable. A blanket in the south pasture. Even in my fucking shower.

Fuck, I was in trouble if I was imagining doing all that with a woman who clearly hated my guts.

"You got Claire out of me," Huck reminded Alice.

Alice's face softened at the mention of Huck's daughter. The woman had been part of the family since before I was born and had stayed on to take care of us after our parents died when I was fifteen. She wasn't a blood relation, but she was definitely Claire's honorary grandmother. "I did. Now get a woman, too."

Huck titled his head back and laughed. Claire's mother was a piece of work and long gone. Huck was better off without her. So was Claire.

Maybe Alice was right in her putting us in this auction. Clearly, Huck and I sucked at picking women. As for Thatcher, no woman had turned out to be a gold digger or shown up pregnant for him, but he was still single, and that was his fatal flaw in Alice's eyes.

"Yes, ma'am," Huck said, appeasing Alice.

"The auction was organized through the community center," she said, picking up the cutting board and sliding the cut carrots into the pot on the stove. "You have to admit it's something different than last year's holiday wreath sale."

It sure as hell was. Selling some holly bows was one thing, selling myself another.

"Rev. Abernathy will be the MC," she added, as if that made it better.

Thatcher laughed. Huck groaned. I did, too, but inwardly. We'd gone to church as kids with our parents, but we'd veered from that flock.

"Are these dates chaperoned then?" Huck asked. "Hang on. This isn't some bait and switch way to have us married then and there, is it?"

I stilled, thinking the possibility was real.

"Huckleberry Manning, did you hit your head? It's a fundraiser not entrapment." Alice gave him the eye again. "Women not just from The Bend will come and bid. I expect some from as far as Helena. It's not often the Manning brothers are up for sale."

Often? More like never. We may have chased skirts in the past, and Huck even may be a father now, but we Manning brothers were selective. At least discreet. We sure as shit didn't kiss and tell.

She eyed the three of us up and down.

We were all over six feet and had our father's broad shoulders, square jaw and blue eyes, but we'd somehow come out with different hair color. My hair was almost black. Huck's was blond and Thatcher was a carrot top. I remembered our father had always said

Momma had two-timed it with a few cowboys to get boys looking so different, but they'd been so much in love that there wasn't a chance either of them had strayed in their marriage. It was a perfect union I wanted for myself, too, but doubted I'd get. I was getting old and, it seemed, only desired for my big bank account or my big dick. Or both.

"I don't need help with my love life," Thatcher said, offering us his sly grin.

Alice humphed and got back to her chopping, moving onto the celery next. The scent of browning meat from the pot on the stove made my stomach growl.

"Love life? No, but you haven't brought a woman home for dinner once," she said to him. "He had a child out of wedlock." She aimed her knife in Huck's direction, and he actually blushed but wasn't ashamed of Claire. Alice loved Claire to death, so her point wasn't about anything but the three of us all having the same single status.

"And you." She turned and offered me a shrewd glance.

"Me?" I asked, setting my hand on my chest. "What have I done?"

She glanced at the peas on my crotch.

"Clearly you're doing it wrong," she countered, full

of sass. "Since you've wasted a bag of my peas trying to get a date."

"After Tina—" I lifted the peas up in the air. "And earlier, you want me to go out and pick up women?"

She frowned, puckered her lips as if the thought of Tina left a sour taste in her mouth. "Pick up? No. Look what that effort did to you. You clearly need to be auctioned off if you can't do it yourself." She turned to her stew pot, a little flustered, then looked at me over her shoulder.

I actually felt my cheeks heat. I felt off my game. I wanted Kelsey. I wanted her to buy me at the auction because I wanted a second chance. Hell, I wanted to know what made her run so hot. But there was no way in hell she'd be buying my sorry ass.

"I'm not raising you boys forever," she continued. "I've told you before, and I'm telling you again, I'm working on moving to be near my sister in Alabama where it's warm all year round."

She'd said that before, and I had a sneaking suspicion she was getting more serious about the plan by the day. Alice had been our rock since our parents had died. She was mother, housekeeper, nurse and had even been chauffeur until I got my license and took over that role.

"You don't want us to pick up random women, but

you're okay with us being auctioned off to the highest bidder?" Huck asked.

"I wasn't trying to pick up a *random* woman," I reminded, trying to make them see that I wasn't a manwhore. "The new preschool teacher's... hell, she's something. I offered to show her around town not my bed."

Alice narrowed her eyes and pursed her lips.

She ignored me and Thatcher and spun about to face Huck. "*You* volunteered—"

"Volunteered? More like shanghaied," Huck cut in, but it did nothing to stop Alice.

"—to be bachelors to raise money for the youth program at the community center. You remember how involved you were as kids."

We'd done little league and a few camping trips. Some dances. I'd even had my first kiss at one of those.

When I'd gone off to college in Missoula, Huck and Thatcher—who were two and four years younger—had done more stuff through the program. Alice was right. It was a worthwhile cause, but I'd rather write them a check than be in an auction, but I didn't dare suggest that. I was the fucking fire chief. I was invested in this town.

"Miss Turnbuckle will be a dream date in comparison to someone like Delilah Mays," Thatcher said then gave an exaggerated shiver. He might be the least... selective but wasn't interested in that piece of work either.

"Delilah?" Huck groaned and went to the fridge, grabbed a mug from the cabinet and poured himself some coffee, which Alice always kept fresh. "She's had her sights set on any one of us since we got hair on our balls."

"Language," Alice warned again, shaking her head in her usual dismay at Huck's crude words.

"What the he—heck, Huck?" I said at the same time, trying not to laugh, even though it was true.

"You have a point there," Alice conceded. "I can't believe she hopped in your bed senior year."

"Hopped in my bed?" I asked, eyes wide. "Alice, she didn't come through the front door. She climbed through the window and stripped herself bare."

Thatcher chuckled. "First time you get a woman in bed, and you can't perform."

I couldn't help but laugh, even though at the time, it was a nightmare. Delilah was beautiful. Had been even back then. Any high schooler's wet dream. But when she surprised you in your bed... my teenage dick had gotten hard at the sight of her perky tits but quickly deflated. For a while, I'd thought she'd broken me.

That fiasco hadn't deterred her much although she'd moved onto Huck and Thatcher. She hadn't climbed in their windows. At least she'd learned that lesson although I was sure she still wanted one of us, all these years of rejection later.

Alice cleared her throat and went over to the stove to turn the burner down, the sizzle of the meat quieting. She knew we weren't virgins, but we sure as shit didn't share where we put our dicks with her.

"She'll give any man stage fright," Huck countered.

"That was over ten years ago. She isn't any better these days," I added although not because I'd ever had her in my bed. Fuck, no. "She was at pick up. Her daughter's just like her. Be glad Claire will be a year ahead in school."

Huck ran a hand over his face and sighed.

"There will be other women bidding besides Delilah," Alice added, steering the conversation back to the bachelor auction. "It's a great way for women to approach you three." She looked us up and down. "You have to admit, between your grouchy faces and your size, you're formidable."

"Can't we just donate money to the program instead?" Huck asked, voicing my thought then taking a swig of coffee. He'd always been the moodiest of the three of us, but we were all equally doomed to this event. Complaining about it wasn't going to make it any better.

"Enough." Alice set her hands on her narrow hips. At close to seventy, she had a straight spine and was as healthy as a horse. Each of us might have almost a hundred pounds on her, but no one messed with Alice. "If Huck can talk about the hair on your balls, then I can talk about the days I used to help you wipe your butts." She paused for effect, which had all three of us squirming. She pointed her knife at us again. "You three will be at the bachelor auction on Friday night. You're being auctioned off to available—and hopefully appealing—women. End of discussion."

3

Two days later

"This is a fucking nightmare," Huck murmured, moving to lean against the wall. We were backstage at the community center, waiting for our turn to be called out and auctioned off. We were all wearing our fanciest duds which amounted to clean jeans and pressed shirts. Thatcher tossed me a breath mint then stuck one in his mouth.

Huck would rather run for the hills than stand

here, and I knew only Alice's wrath was keeping him —and me—from doing so.

"Dude, have you seen all the women out there?" Thatcher asked, going to peek around the corner to check out the audience. *He* seemed much more eager. Hell, he could have my date and probably Huck's, too.

Clapping and lady shouts bounced off the concrete walls. Another guy bit the dust. The turnout was more than I'd ever imagined. The building was used for everything from basketball to swimming to seniors' programs, plus designed to handle all kinds of town events, but a bachelor auction was a first. There had to be a hundred women out there, and the estrogen levels were through the roof.

About fifteen guys had been wrangled into trading dates for a charitable donation. We knew a few personally from growing up together or around town, but others must have been pulled from around the county.

Based on the bids the first three guys had been "sold" for, it showed how eager some women were to help the kid's program. Or to find a date.

Thatcher came over, slapped me on the shoulder. "Have your balls dropped out of your throat yet?"

He grinned, and I glared.

Huck grinned. "Dude, you've got it bad."

I did. I'd spent the past two days thinking about the gorgeous redhead who'd shot me down.

"I need to know what I did. What I said to set her off," I said to them. Again.

"You need to steer clear of crazy," Huck told me.

"You want to date her?" Thatcher replied, eyeing me.

"I have no idea what I want to do with the woman," I replied. Date? I had no fucking clue. Maybe I hit my head when she took me to the floor because why the fuck would I want to track down a woman who very clearly wanted nothing to do with me? Who hated my guts.

Was she a challenge? Was she insane? Was I?

My answer only made Huck laugh, which was the first time since we'd walked into the community center. "Only you'd want to claim a woman who had bigger balls that you."

Claim? The idea didn't sit too badly. But I still had to find her. I had to know. She was hot to anger which only made me wonder if she got hot fast for other reasons.

The last thing I wanted was to make her upset. I winced, hoping whenever I saw her again, I could set things straight. A smarter man would just steer clear, so that made me as dumb as a box of rocks.

"Gonna be tough to make this right if you take another woman out on a date," Thatcher said, tipping his head toward the stage.

I glared at him. "Whoever buys me isn't getting anything more from me than coffee. With Kelsey, I want to..." I stopped talking because I had no idea what I wanted to do with her. Well, I did, but why?

"Whatever you do, wear a cup," Huck joked, and Thatcher tossed his head back and laughed, even slapped his thigh.

She was so fucking pretty. Petite with curves that went on for miles. She wasn't flashy like Delilah and Tracy had been in their designer duds and fake eyelashes as they'd watched their girls play. Kelsey's simple outfit had only accentuated her pale skin, those full lips. The swell of her small but perky tits. The streak of paint on her shirt had shown she didn't mind getting dirty, and the way she'd talked gently to the diva-in-training Tamara said she was a fucking rock star with kids.

Within five minutes, I'd figured out I wanted her. I needed to get her from *no fucking way* to *yes, fuck me please.* From kneeing me in the balls to cupping them in her palm while she sucked my dick.

Here I was backstage, ready to be some woman's

date for a charity, and I was losing my shit. For a preschool teacher.

I ran a hand over my face, watched as another guy had his turn.

Shit. I didn't want a random date. I wanted Kelsey.

I ran a hand over my hair, which, per Alice's instructions, was neatly combed.

"Manning, you're up next," Rev. Abernathy called, then stuck his balding head around the curtain. "Oh great, all three of you are here. Which one of you wants to go first?"

Huck, Thatcher and I glanced at each other. Huck tapped his nose, then Thatcher in our usual game of "nose goes", where whoever touches last must do the task. In this case, auctioned to a noisy and rowdy group of women. I sighed, resigning myself to what was about to happen. "That would be me."

The minister disappeared.

"Let's get this over with," I muttered then followed the man of the Lord out onto the stage.

————

KELSEY

. . .

I'D WAITED for the call from Irene to tell me I'd been
fired. After I left the preschool the other day, I'd gone
to the laundromat to wash the small pile of clothes I'd
had in the trunk of my car. While I'd lost my shit.
Then I'd gone to the community center, where I'd
cried my eyes out in the shower in the ladies' locker
room at what I'd done. Then onto the grocery store to
buy a few frozen dinners. When I'd unlocked the
backdoor of the preschool with my key so I could heat
up my meal in the microwave and get some sleep, I'd
almost cried in relief. Not that Irene would have had
the locks changed, but I'd been irrational in my fear of
Sawyer Manning wanting me gone. Of having me
fired.

I wouldn't have blamed him. My behavior had
been worse than Tamara's.

Sawyer must not have done anything because it
had been two days since I'd kneed his junk, and I
hadn't heard a peep. Sarah Jane hadn't said a word and
when I'd worked with Irene this morning she had only
asked me with her usual concern about how I was
doing with getting my deposit money together. It was
as if the confrontation had never happened. Of course,
Claire hadn't attended either day since, so I hadn't had
a run-in again. There always next week, which
still had me freaking out.

When Sarah Jane invited me to the bachelor auction—what she'd said was *the* event of the summer —I'd met up with her and Irene in the auditorium. It was then I finally realized that to everyone else besides me and Sawyer Manning, *nothing had happened.*

There had to be a hundred women here, all seated at round tables, laughing and clapping, hooting and hollering as one man after another was auctioned off.

I didn't have a dime to my name, so I had no intention of buying myself a date. Irene was married, so she was here just for the fun as well. Sarah Jane was my age and single, offering a play-by-play commentary on every guy and every woman who bid on them. She'd grown up here and knew every bit of juicy gossip. Because of that, she'd said she probably wasn't going to bid on a guy although she was going to keep her options open just in case.

I was thankful for their friendship. Irene's kindness in my predicament.

The minister—an odd choice for an MC for a bachelor auction—announced the latest guy. He came out on stage with a big, but nervous smile.

"Owen Zerwig. I went to school with his sister," Sarah Jane said. The room was so loud that she didn't need to talk quietly. In fact, she had to speak up for me to hear.

He had sandy blond hair and was a good looking guy. Sturdy work boots, pressed Wranglers and a plaid shirt. He had a full head of hair and from what the minister was saying, owned a home and was gainfully employed.

A catch.

"He's a good man," Irene added, tipping her chin toward Owen. "Handsome, too. Why don't you put a bid in?" she asked Sarah Jane.

She shook her head, her cute chin length bob swinging around her cheeks. "I've seen his penis."

My mouth fell open as she answered that as if she was asking me to pass the salt. Irene's eyes bugged out.

"We were four and playing in a kiddie pool, but still, I've seen it."

"I'm sure it's... bigger now," Irene commented, trying very hard to keep a straight face.

Sarah Jane and I looked at each other then burst out laughing.

"Oh look, Delilah's bidding," Irene said.

Sarah Jane and I turned at the mention of the preschool mother. She was just as put together as the other day on the playground although her top was a little tighter and her eye makeup a touch heavier.

"Isn't she married?" I asked, picking up my plastic

cup for a drink. This was an alcohol-free event, so there were water stations in the corners of the room.

They shook their heads. "Never put a ring on it," Sarah Jane commented.

"She'll probably hold out for one of the Manning boys," Irene added, taking a glance at her cell phone then sitting it on the table.

My heart leapt at the name, and I coughed on the sip I'd just taken. She eyed me with concern but continued. "Rich and gorgeous. A double draw for Delilah."

"For most women," Sarah Jane added. "I heard they're being auctioned tonight, too."

Irene nodded. "They're good boys. I'm friends with their housekeeper. She volunteered all three of them for the event. I wish I'd been a fly on the wall when she'd told them."

I thought of Sawyer Manning. How big he was. How gorgeous. "There are three of them?"

Sarah Jane fanned herself. "Yup. Sawyer, Huck and Thatcher."

"From Mark Twain?" I asked.

Irene nodded. "Nice job. Not everyone picks up on that. Their mother had a thing for his books."

"They're all equally gorgeous," Sarah Jane added

then bit her lip. "I might have to bid on one of them. Not sure which."

"Dark, fair or ginger?" Irene asked her with a sly grin.

Sarah Jane considered, tapping her chin. "I wish the Mannings were like ice cream scoops, and I could have all three."

I was totally confused, and I set my cup down, held up my hand. "Hang on. One of them is Claire Manning's father."

They nodded.

"But he can't be in the auction. He's married."

"Sold!" the minister shouted, and the ladies clapped. Owen blushed and grinned from the stage. The woman who won him—not Delilah—stood, and he went down the steps to meet her. I watched but didn't pay them any attention. My mind was on the fact that there were three Manning brothers. If the other two looked like Sawyer... wow.

"No. Huck's not married. Not sure the scoop there but—"

I gripped Sarah Jane's arm, stared at her wide eyed. "Huck?"

She frowned, looked down at my hold. "Yeah. Huck Manning is Claire's dad."

I licked my suddenly dry lips. "Then... then who's Sawyer Manning?"

Cocking her head to the side, she looked to me then her eyes brightened. "The oldest. Oh, you met him at pickup the other day. He's Claire's uncle."

Uncle. Not father.

"And he's... a bachelor?" I squeaked.

Irene laughed. "All three of them. Huck never married. Alice wants them to settle down."

Holy shit.

Sawyer Manning was single. He wasn't married. And his turn was just called by the minister.

Ladies clapped, a few catcalled as the tall, dark and handsome cowboy walked out on stage. My blood pressure went to stroke point just staring up at him. Yeah, this was the guy I'd kneed in the balls. For no reason.

Oh my god.

"What do you ladies think of this fine bachelor?" the minister asked the crowd, and they responded by even louder clapping and shouting. I agreed with them completely. He was a stunning example of a red-blooded cowboy.

Sawyer Manning, in jeans, polished work boots and a crisp blue shirt, took off his Stetson and ran a hand over the back of his neck. While he was smiling, he didn't seem too thrilled about all the attention. Or eager for a date like Owen before him had.

Sawyer had been into me the other day.

Oh my God.

He'd asked me out. I'd kneed him in the crotch.

I had to apologize. To make things right.

"Shall we start the bidding?" When the applause died down, the minister said, "Let's begin with fifty dollars."

The bids began, fast and furious, one after the other.

"He's the oldest of the three," Sarah Jane commented. "I've met him once. Super nice. I'm not sure if I'd pick him or Thatcher. He's the red head. He'll come up next or last, I assume."

I vaguely nodded but watched the women bid from all around the room. Including Delilah.

My gaze returned to Sawyer. He stood tall and... huge, holding his Stetson against his chest. Looking at him now gave me the same thrill as the other day. My heart raced. My mouth watered. There was something about him that called to me. That made me *want.*

Every time Delilah called out a bid, his jaw ticked. While he stood casually, I couldn't miss the way his fingers clenched then released. He wasn't happy.

"This just might be the way she'll get that date

she's always wanted," Sarah Jane said, pointing to Delilah. She was smiling, a predatory gleam in her eye I couldn't miss even from across the room. "It's telling that she has to pay to do so."

"You're right," I told her. "I heard her talking about him the other day at pick-up."

Sarah Jane frowned. "No fun for Sawyer."

Sawyer had told me he didn't like her. Said he'd known her his whole life, that he hadn't been into her all this time. If he was right that Tamara took after her mother... a date with Delilah would be miserable. And if she got those manicured talons into him...

It wasn't fair.

"Three hundred!" Delilah called, raising the bid another fifty dollars.

The minister looked around the room waiting for other bidders. It had tapered down and petered out at that large amount for one date.

Sawyer remained still, his body tense. He'd volunteered for this, his time given freely for a good cause. Hundreds of dollars to the kids' program was amazing, but while it would come from Delilah's bank account, it would be costly to Sawyer to spend the time with the woman he didn't like.

"Going once."

I couldn't let that happen.

"Going twice."

I owed it to Sawyer Manning for what I'd done.

"Five hundred dollars," I shouted.

Every head in the room turned to look at me.

Irene gasped, and Sarah Jane stared at me wide eyed. Her mouth even hung open. I'd surprised them, and it seemed every other person in the auditorium.

Sawyer Manning's gaze whipped to mine. Met. Held.

My nipples went instantly hard.

"Sold!"

Everyone clapped, but I didn't hear it as I stared at Sawyer. My heart was in my throat, and my hands were clammy.

"Um, Kelsey," Sarah Jane murmured then shook my arm. I wasn't turning my gaze for anything. "What... why... you just won Sawyer Manning."

"I know," I said, equally thrilled and panicked. What had I done?

"Honey, I know we said he was attractive and all, but the money..." Irene said, her words tapering off. She was the only one who knew of my circumstances. Even Sarah Jane didn't know I slept at the preschool. I was very careful, keeping my things like a toothbrush in a bag and tucking it in one of the higher cabinets. The small bed in the preschool's back room I kept neatly made. The personal possessions my bitch ex-roommate hadn't taken were tucked in a mini-storage locker on the edge of town. My clothes in the trunk of my car. What Irene was reminding me—because I'd clearly lost my mind—was that I didn't have the money to pay for the bid. She didn't care that I'd bought a bachelor but worried that I'd made my situation obvious by not being able to follow through. It would be embarrassing for me and for Sawyer. The charity would be short money some other woman, even Delilah, would have gladly given.

I nodded then admitted, "I know, I didn't think."

Irene chuckled. "Honey, you're not the first woman to have her brain cells fried over a Manning."

Sawyer hopped down from the stage, skipping the steps and sauntered over—yeah, that was what it was called when a hot cowboy walked my way—not looking anywhere but at me.

I licked my lips and swallowed hard, unable to tear my eyes from him.

"But why? Besides the obvious," Sarah Jane wondered.

"I kneed him the balls," I admitted, not looking at either of my friends.

Irene kept right on laughing.

"You what?" Sarah Jane practically shouted, but I

wasn't going to answer because Sawyer was beside me, setting his hat on his head.

I had to tilt my chin back to look up at him. He held his hand out, and I took it.

He gave a little tug and pulled me to my feet then leaned down. Before I could even question what he was doing, he tossed me over his shoulder and carried me out of the room.

4

SAWYER

THE WAY I took her out of the room probably wasn't the best idea. It might have been the fireman's carry, and I was the fire chief, but there was no fire. If I wanted the town to stay out of my love life, that wasn't the way to do it. But when it was Kelsey who had shouted out the winning bid, my inner caveman had taken over. I'd resigned myself to taking Delilah for coffee. In the morning. At the cafe on Main Street that had lots of witnesses, so she'd keep her hands off me. But then Kelsey, out of the blue, had shouted out a higher bid. Rev. Abernathy had called *Sold* faster than

Delilah could respond, thank God. Literally and figuratively.

I'd gotten exactly what I wanted. A date with Kelsey. Was I insane? I was going to sure as shit find out. As soon as I'd found her in the crowd, I hadn't looked away. How had I missed her? That wild red hair. That creamy skin. Those full lips. How gorgeous she was.

She might have been the one to buy me, but she was mine now. Why I wanted her I had no fucking idea. Maybe I was a masochist. Maybe I wanted a challenge. I wanted to know if her pussy had the same fiery curls as on her head.

Besides all that, we had shit to figure out, like why she'd kneed me in the balls. Why she'd done that then bought me at an auction.

With my arm banded about her thighs, I walked straight out of the building and didn't put her down until we were beside my truck. While the parking lot was full, it was deserted since the auction was still going on. If Huck and Thatcher were the only two guys left, it wouldn't be for much longer.

Summer nights were long in The Bend, the sun just having set behind the mountains. The town was nestled in a broad valley, the downtown built around a crook in the river. It was quaint and picturesque, but the only thing I could see was the woman I'd just placed back on her feet.

Her hair was long and wild about her face, the red tendrils seemingly having a mind of their own. Very Medusa-like. A pink flush brightened her cheeks, and most likely, anger brightened her green eyes.

She wore jeans with a pale blue top—no paint smudges—and leather sandals. Simple, but the lack of flash only showcased the soft swell of her lush tits, the curve of her hips. She was just naturally pretty. Hell, she wasn't trying. I wasn't sure if she really even knew just how fucking stunning she was.

She glanced around, as if figuring out where we were, then looked back at me. Her chin went up, so she could look me in the eye, but I had a feeling it was also because she was pissed off, although the slight play of her lips gave her away. She *liked* being manhandled, at least by me..

And yet, I had no idea why her sass made me hot for her.

"I could have walked, you know," she said, setting her hands on her hips and cocking her head.

I grinned because somehow this little firecracker's ire intrigued me. "And you could have kneed me in the balls again."

Her gaze drifted away, and she smoothed her

hands down the front of her jeans. She licked her lips, which had me stifle a groan and think of baseball stats, so I didn't have a zipper mark in my dick. "Yeah, sorry about that."

"Are you?" I asked, tipping my hat back to study her even more closely.

"Are you married?" she countered. That chin tipped up again. There was a little divot there that I wanted to tuck my thumb into while I kissed her.

"No."

"Then I'm sorry. But I could have walked."

"I was helping you from the room. I'm a fireman. I do the fireman's carry."

She looked me up and down as if surprised. "I don't need your help."

"But I needed yours?"

"Did you want to be bought by Delilah?"

I pinched my lips together, ran a hand over the back of my neck.

"You should be thanking me," she said.

I tilted my head down to look her in the eye. Smiled. "Me? Thanking you? I'm the one who had to put frozen peas on his balls."

"I *saved* you from a crazy woman."

I cocked an eyebrow. "Are you sure?"

It was her turn to purse her lips because she

caught on—we weren't talking about Delilah any longer. The glare she gave me would've singed a lesser man, which only made my smile spread into a grin

That fierceness made me laugh. What the fuck was it with this woman? Sassy as fuck. She gave as good as she got. We'd talked in circles where I was about to *thank* her for something although I wasn't quite sure what any longer.

"You don't like to be hit on by married men," I said, hopefully cutting to the crux of this whole mess.

"Would you?" She crossed her arms over her chest, which I guessed was to make her look put out. Instead, it pushed her tits up and made me want to see if her bra was lacy or something plain. I guessed lace. Lavender lace.

Fuck.

"What?" I asked, forgetting what we were talking about.

She sighed. "Would you want to be hit on by a married woman?"

Ah. She'd thought I was married, and Claire was mine.

I crossed my arms over my chest, mimicking her. "Why don't we get this out in the open right now. I'm not married. Never have been. I don't have a girlfriend. Hell, I haven't even dated anyone in forever. That's why Alice volunteered me for the auction. As for Claire, she's my niece. Okay?"

She nodded and scrunched up her face in a cute kind of wince. Peeked up at me. I had no idea eyelashes could be so red. "I don't like cheaters."

I studied her, saw that fire in her gaze again. This time, it wasn't directed at me. No, it was some internal anger. Someone had hurt her before, and it didn't take a rocket scientist to figure out a guy had done her wrong. A married one. I didn't blame her for being cautious.

"Yeah, I got that." When she didn't say anything, I continued. "If you're my woman, you're it," I told her, pointing at her then at my chest. "Meaning I don't stray. You don't like cheaters, I don't like liars."

Tina had lied about her interest in me. She'd lied about her involvement in our relationship. I'd bought her a ring, was ready to commit to her, but she hadn't wanted me. She'd wanted my money, not the simple life of a firefighter's wife. The Manning ranch was huge and went back generations. She'd wanted to play Lady of the Manor or some shit. I loved the family land and money, but it didn't define me.

Kelsey wasn't Tina, but I was going to make it clear right from the start because it seemed she liked things clearly spelled out.

Her eyes widened at my statement, those arched brows winging up. "Okay," she replied then gave me a nod.

"You're the one who bought me, so I'm your man," I added, and I couldn't help but grin. I liked the sound of that. I also liked the look on her face when I said those words, knowing she'd react.

A warm breeze kicked up and played with her curls. I wanted to tuck them behind her ear. For a second, I resisted. Fuck it.

I reached out and pushed the locks back and watched as one slid free. She frowned, that green gaze narrowing. Since she hadn't flinched or stepped away, I assumed the look was because of my words not my action.

"You're my... what?" The eyebrows went up again, and her pale cheeks flushed pink. I had to wonder what else on her body was such a pretty shade of pink.

Fuck yeah. There was that hint of fire that, for some crazy reason, made my dick hard. Why couldn't I be hot for Sally Jensen or Lily Sanchez? They were sweet, kind women who I'd grown up with. Single. They were the kind of women who needed a guy to rescue a cat. I did that shit, even got paid for it. Alice would be off my back if I was into either of them. But no. I had to be attracted to the only woman in town who'd kneed me in the balls and asked me to thank her for it and had a smile on her face while doing so.

I shifted my stance, my jeans suddenly very uncomfortable. Yeah, I was losing it. Especially when I said, "You bought me. I'm yours." I thumbed over my shoulder toward the building.

"Yeah, um... about that." She bit her lip and studiously studied the snaps on the front of my shirt.

I waited. Not because I was patient but because I was thinking about that plump lip and all the things I wanted to do with it. And that was only one tiny part of her. There was so much of her to explore.

"Like I said, I bid to save you from Delilah," she admitted.

"That's the only reason?" I asked, giving her a wink.

Her green eyes narrowed again, and she set a finger over my lips. "After you came out on stage, Irene and Sarah Jane told me you weren't married, and I remembered what you said the other day about Delilah. How you disliked her. After what I'd done—" She dropped her hand and pointed toward my crotch which only got me even harder. "—I couldn't let you get stuck on a horrible date."

"It would've been horrible," I admitted. "I'd rather get snagged on barbed wire and spend an evening getting a tetanus shot in the ER than go out with Delilah."

That made her grin although I was dead serious. "That bad?"

"That fucking bad." I remembered her laying in my bed waiting for me. I tried not to shudder.

Her smile slipped. "The thing is, I... I wasn't thinking. I was so surprised when they said you were single. I mean, I figured you just *had* to be married."

I wasn't sure what she meant by that, and she plowed on.

"Then I saw Delilah's face when she'd bid the highest. All I wanted to do was save you from her, but I... I don't have five hundred dollars."

I stared at her. Fuck, this woman. She was loyal and devoted and didn't even understand that. She'd saved me.

I was the one who usually did the saving, so everything about this... this with her was weird. And yet I reached around and cupped the back of her neck. Held her in place as I lowered my head and kissed her. Not rough, just a gentle swipe, but fuck, I'd been wanting to do that since I first laid eyes on her.

She was still at first but then relaxed, and that... that had my dick leaking pre-cum, even though it had felt the wrath of her knee the other day. The feel of her giving over to me was even more triumphant after how much she'd fought. Not me, but this pull between us. She'd felt it right from the start, too, otherwise she wouldn't have been so pissed when I'd asked her out. Fuck.

"This wasn't part of the deal," she murmured against my lips.

"Do you want me to stop?" I asked.

"No. God no." Then she kissed me right back. Her lips were soft and full. Her scent was flowery. Her taste, when she gasped and I took the opportunity for my tongue to explore, was sugary and sweet.

She moaned.

I groaned.

We were in the community center parking lot. Not the place to take things further, so I pulled back and set my forehead to hers but kept my hand in place at her nape.

"What was that for?" she whispered. Her green eyes were bright but blurry. Her lips swollen and slick. And now the bright color on her cheeks was from arousal.

"I love that you weren't thinking when you saved me from Delilah. You weren't thinking with your head."

She stared at me, and that little V formed in her

brow again. "It wasn't with my heart. I don't even know you. What else do I think with?"

When she licked her lip, I stepped close, close enough so her soft body was pressed against my hard one. With our height difference, my dick was pressed against her belly. My leg settled between hers, and my thigh nestled into the apex of her thighs.

A gasp escaped her lips, and she shifted her hips, which only rubbed her core on me.

"Your pussy."

Her mouth fell open, and then she pulled back. I turned my body slightly, prepared for another knee since my talk was crude. Hopefully not too crude that would set her off again. She moved a few feet back and stared at me, covered her lips with her fingers. I stared at her right back. Waited.

Yeah, this was happening. I wanted her. She wanted me, even though she may not have realized it until now. She didn't have to say the words *I want you.* Her actions, winning me at the auction to protect me, spoke for her loud and clear, even if she didn't realize it.

She was fierce and shit, I had no idea that was such a turn on. I wasn't done with her, not by a long shot.

I crooked my finger. "Thank you for saving me from Delilah. As for the money, I'll square up with

Alice and the organizers. Come on. Let's get out of here before the auction's over. I'll show you around town."

She cocked her head to the side, bit her lip again. "The other day, I thought that was a euphemism."

I tilted my head back and laughed. This woman... fuck, I was in trouble.

"Sugar, you won't have to wonder if I'm taking you to my bed." I let my gaze rake over every inch of her. "You'll know. And you'll want it too."

———

KELSEY

AN HOUR LATER, we were sitting on the open tailgate of Sawyer's pickup truck in the parking lot of Frosty Frills, the town's ice cream stand. He'd gotten me a chocolate and vanilla swirl soft-serve cone and a vanilla one for himself. I swung my feet back and forth and enjoyed the simple pleasure of a summer night and a cool treat.

I'd been pinching my pennies so hard these days— ramen noodles and cheap microwavable entrees were my staples—that the ice cream was so good. Since there was a hot guy included, it was even better. This one though, I wasn't sure why. Why did he drive me crazy and make me want to kiss him some more all at the same time?

He'd actually driven me around town, pointing out the sights, which weren't many. The high school. Library. Town hall. While he was confident enough to have flung me over his shoulder in an auditorium full of women, it seemed he didn't quite know what to do with me. I loved that he'd pointed out the post office on our drive, but... yeah. A little odd. Especially since every one of those places had a sign out front, and I hadn't needed a tour guide for any of them.

I was sure he knew that. I was sure he knew that I knew that. It was a good thing there wasn't a quiz when we'd parked for ice cream because my thoughts had been toggling between *That kiss!* and *He's not married!*

Maybe his brain cells had been fried and a drive-around was all he'd been able to do. Maybe he was as nice as Irene had said, and a tour of town was a date for him. The chemistry though, the undeniable sizzle in the cab of his truck, had been hard to miss. It was that... tension that made a really average tour of The Bend foreplay.

Although that meant we were going to have sex

next... oh my God. My pussy was thinking for me, as he'd said. That kiss had been a warm-up, a taste of what it would be like between us if we did more. Hell, not a warm-up. I'd been warmed up ever since I saw him at the playground. The way he'd carried me out of the community center had made my nipples instantly hard, and my panties were ruined. *Ruined.*

Not that I was going to tell him that. I didn't need to be rescued, and clearly, he was the kind of guy who did that being a fireman and all. Rescuing people was in his job description.

I was still hot from it, and the ice cream wasn't doing anything to cool me off. Watching Sawyer lick a cone had me wondering how dexterous his tongue was at other tasks. Even more foreplay.

It had been a while for me. I wasn't going to think back to being with Tom, the asshole, but I could compare. I got more out of the kiss with Sawyer than I had the entire time I'd been with Tom.

"I like your truck," I said, patting the open tailgate.

"Thanks. It was my mom's. The other day you said you moved here from Colorado," he said, making small talk. His jeans stretched taut over his thighs, and since he was so tall, his work boots almost touched the pavement. It wasn't that he was so big, it was that I felt so small, so feminine sitting next to him.

"Yup," I replied.

With him sitting this close, it was hard not to study him. The dark hair, the slight crook to his nose. The full lips that I remembered the feel of against mine. He must've shaved before the auction because there wasn't a hint of scruff. His square jaw was very distracting. Even the way his Adam's apple bobbed when he swallowed was attractive.

"I... well, I followed a guy up here. *That* didn't work out."

"You sure it didn't work out for the best?" he asked.

I couldn't help but frown as I remembered standing on Tom's doorstep to surprise him only to have it opened by an eight year old who'd called for Daddy. I'd realized then and there I had behaved just like my mother. Unlike her, I didn't break up families. I never wanted to be the *other woman.*

"I'm very sure," I replied, frowning.

"It got you here with me. I'd say it worked out just fine."

My gaze whipped up to his, and I had no idea how to respond. He just gave his cone a lick, which had me staring.

"Have you always wanted to work with kids?" Huh? The guy was giving me conversational whiplash.

I took a second then cleared my throat. "Always. I

got my degree in early childhood education and like working with the little ones the best." I couldn't help but smile.

"You're good with them."

I felt warm beneath his praise, and I shyly tucked my hair back behind my ear. "I love it. The excitement and curiosity. They're always eager to just... be happy."

"You aren't?" Cocking his head, he studied me. I was amazed how that hat of his stayed on, as if it was a part of him.

I shrugged. "Life's not always easy."

There was no way I was telling this guy all my issues. He'd be running away if he knew just how stupid I'd been and how much I'd lost. I certainly wasn't going to tell him my troubles, so he'd help me out. I just needed a few more paychecks, and I'd be able to get the little efficiency apartment in the four-plex near the bowling alley. I'd gotten myself into a mess, and I was going to get myself out of it. On my own.

I'd be back on my feet after falling hard. That wasn't the right term. I'd tripped and skidded across asphalt face first.

He nodded, as if filing my answer away. "Just so you know, this isn't our auction date."

"No?"

"I haven't taken a girl here for a date since I was sixteen. I've upped my game since then."

I guessed he was in his early thirties. I wasn't going to think of all the women he'd been with since high school. "No doubt." I wiped my mouth with a paper napkin, unsure if it was ice cream or drool I was blotting because he'd definitely aged well. I could only imagine how many hearts he'd crushed back in the day when he'd had a cute baby face. "I'm... um, sorry about kneeing you."

This time when I said it, I really meant it. He was a nice guy. He made me crazy, thus the ball kneeing.

He turned to face me, his thigh now nudging mine. "I understand why you did it. While my balls don't agree, I like that you stood up for yourself. I will say this, for the sake of the chance of future children, you got a question... ask. I'll tell you the truth."

God, he was nice. And that was scarier than the possibility of him being married. I didn't understand nice.

"Okay," I whispered. What else was there to say?

"I guess there's a story behind your reaction."

The ice cream soured on my tongue. "As I told you, I don't like cheaters. *Married* cheaters," I clarified, as if there were two different levels of being a dick.

We were quiet for a minute, and Sawyer had begun to take bites out of his cone.

"If getting ice cream isn't our date then what is?" I asked.

He glanced at me then waved to a couple who climbed from their car to get in line.

"I'm sure the reverend had something just like this in mind. Rated-G and chaperoned." He tipped his head to a family with two little kids getting in line.

"Not you?" I asked, licking a drip from the rim of the cone.

His dark eyes followed the motion, and he cleared his throat.

"I like a good cone, but I like the taste of other things I can lick with my mouth and tongue even more."

Holy shit.

He dropped that word porn like a sexy bomb and went back to licking his soft serve and taking bites out of that sugar cone. I'd never thought I'd be jealous of ice cream before.

When I just stared at him, letting my soft serve melt—and my pussy drip—he looked to me. It was full dark now, but while the parking lot was well lit, deep shadows were cast across Sawyer's face. I couldn't miss his slow smirk, the way he knew his banter had hit its mark: my pussy.

I shouldn't be getting involved with this guy. He was too... everything. Irene and Sarah Jane both agreed. He was also too hard to resist. I should be pushing him away, but I wanted this. Whatever *this* was. I wasn't looking for a guy to take over my life. To *be* my life. I just wanted a little sex with the hottest cowboy around. Was there anything wrong with that?

When my mind and my pussy came to the same answer—no—I grinned. Two could play his game, and I wanted in. He was testing me to gauge my interest, to see how far I'd go on this first not-date. He wanted me. That kiss had been proof. And the innuendo? Wow.

The choice was mine to make how this night happened. I could switch topics and talk about the weather or any number of non-sexy topics, but that wasn't what I wanted.

The second he'd walked up to the playground the other day, I'd been attracted. Wanted. Perhaps that was why I'd been so angry when I thought he was married. It had scared the shit out of me that I'd felt like that, petrified I really was the kind of woman I refused to be.

He wasn't married. Besides his word, in a town as small as The Bend, he couldn't get on stage and be auctioned off as a bachelor if he wasn't one. Not when a minister was the fudging MC. No, Sawyer Manning was single. He'd been into me the other day and was into me now. Why, after I'd kneed him in the balls, I had no idea.

These feelings weren't anything more than that... *feelings.*

And the interest was *very* mutual.

"Yeah, me too," I countered. "I like to lick just the tip, but then make sure I swirl my tongue around the whole thing."

His gaze whipped to mine, and his smile dropped away completely. He took off his hat, ran a hand over his dark hair, then tucked it back on his head. I'd totally surprised him, and I bit back a smile.

He cleared his throat, and the corner of his mouth tipped up. "I imagine you're very diligent with your *cone* licking."

I shrugged, trying to be nonchalant, even though I wanted to climb him like a tree. "I mean, I think it's important to pay attention to the entire *cone*," I added. "It's most enjoyable that way."

His eyes flared with heat. A nerve ticked in his jaw. Yeah, I couldn't miss that.

"We shouldn't just talk about my cone." He tipped his head in my direction. "What about *your* cone? I'd love to get your cone to melt because I want to find out how much it drips," he said, his voice an octave deeper than before.

Oh. My. God. My own cone—and not the one in my hand—sure as shit was dripping now.

"It's important to lick it everywhere," he said, leaning closer, his voice going quieter. "Even the rim of the cone. Eventually to dip inside."

My mouth hung open as I stared at him, imagining it all. My pussy clenched, wanting some of that licking.

I wasn't sure if I shifted closer or if he had, but now his warm breath fanned my neck. "Kelsey, I want to lick *your* cone. See how much I've made you melt and drip. Will you let me?"

I whimpered, then nodded. "What about you?"

"If you lick my cone now, it'll melt way too fucking fast for fun. I told you earlier you'd know when I took you to my bed. It's now. I just need to hear the words that you want to be there, sugar."

He was as primed as me. If we weren't in a parking lot filled with teenagers and families getting a Friday night treat, I'd have let him take me in the back of his pickup. Right here. Right fucking now.

I squirmed and said, "Yes."

5

S AWYER

I TUCKED Kelsey back into the truck at hard-dick speed, and we'd turned out of the lot before I even processed more than *must get in Kelsey now.*

At the four-way stop in the center of town, my dick let my brain think for a second. "I don't even know where the fuck I'm going," I admitted. "The ranch is ten miles out of town."

I met Kelsey's green eyes, saw the heat and haste in them.

"Your place?" I asked. I hoped she lived nearby because my bed was too fucking far away.

"Um... the preschool."

My eyebrows shot up. "Excuse me?"

She pointed to the right. "It's two blocks that way. There's a bed in the back room. No one's there until Monday."

She had me at *two blocks away.*

I flicked my blinker and headed in that direction and parked in one of the empty spots on the back side of the building. I hopped out, but Kelsey didn't wait for me to help her down. For once, I didn't give a shit because she had her key out and was opening the door by the time I caught up with her.

She didn't reach for the light switch. Instead, she spun around and reached for me. Well, not reached. More like launched herself at me. I caught her with my hands on her ass, her legs coming around my waist and hooking at my back. Her hand came up and tipped my hat off.

I couldn't help but grin at her eagerness.

This was where I'd first seen Kelsey, and I'd had dirty thoughts about what I wanted to do with her right from the start, but I'd never, ever thought about doing any of them at the preschool.

It was Friday night. After hours. There were no kids around. We could do whatever we wanted, and I wanted to do a whole hell of a lot. This was going to be fast and hard. Wild. I'd get her in my bed and take my time with her. Later.

Now, I kissed the hell out of her as I spun her around and pressed her into the wall. She was so fucking soft and warm, her sweet scent filling my head. She tasted like chocolate and vanilla. I couldn't help the groan that escaped at just holding her in my arms.

"This doesn't mean anything," she murmured then kissed me some more.

I smiled as she gripped the front of my shirt and held on tight.

"Sure," I replied.

She was so small in comparison to me, so feminine. I rolled my hips once, rubbed my hard length against the very center of her. She tipped her head back and moaned, and I kissed down the line of her jaw and to her neck. Breathed her in. Licked the flavor from her skin. Rolled my hips again just so I could hear those sexy-as-fuck sounds she made.

Her hands went to my shirt, tugged the snaps open. Then her soft hands were roaming my chest and when a fingernail lightly brushed over my nipple, that was it. I was too far gone for her.

"Where's the bed?" I practically growled. Her

mouth was buried in my neck, and I had a feeling I was going to have a hickey before we were done.

She didn't stop whatever sucking and licking she was doing with her mouth to stick her arm out and point.

I turned us, strode into the back room. There was enough glow from the streetlights to be able to see, but I wasn't turning any overhead ones on because the preschool didn't have blinds. I wanted Kelsey all to myself. This wasn't going to be a peep show for anyone who walked by.

Before I could get to the small bed in the corner, she cupped me through my jeans, and I changed direction. The wall was closer, and her hand was on my dick. *On. My. Dick.*

"Is that all you?" she asked.

"My dick? Yeah, that's all me." Just the press of those fingers had me close to coming. "Fuck." I hadn't picked up a woman in a long time. Hadn't been this crazed, this insane to get inside hot pussy. Kelsey was making me lose my shit, and I fucking loved it.

I set her on her feet, so she was propped against the wall. When I knew she wasn't going to fall over or crumple to the floor, I dropped to my knees and made quick work of her jeans, pushing them down over her hips, taking her panties with them.

The fabric bunched around her thighs, and I didn't wait another second. I hadn't been lying when I said I wanted to lick her. That I liked to swirl my tongue around the tip, then get my whole mouth on her. So I did just that.

"Still doesn't mean anything?" I asked, licking my lips.

"Sawyer!" she cried. That was what I thought. She was as into this as me.

She sure as fuck wouldn't have gone through with the auction if she felt nothing. If I meant nothing. She was nicer than she thought. Felt more than she shared. She couldn't hide it from me. But I wasn't going to tell her this now.

Fuck no. I pulled back then, looked up at her in the dim light and grinned. Licked my lips.

"I love your body." The scent of her pussy was driving me wild. I had her taste on my tongue, sugary sweet. Perfection. "This pussy's mine."

"Then why did you stop?"

"I only want to hear you calling my name. Or God. Otherwise, you're talking too much."

"If I'm talking too much, then you're not doing it right."

I looked up at her, narrowed my eyes.

She looked equal parts aroused and smug. While I

was now going to get her to come like it was my fucking job, I was also going to wipe that look off her face.

"Challenge fucking accepted, sugar."

She didn't reply, only tangled her fingers in my hair and pushed my face back into her pussy. I grinned for a split second before I got back to work, licking and learning every inch of her.

Her hips shifted and writhed with impatience because her jeans were in the way. I pulled back and got her jeans and panties down her legs. Kelsey helped by toeing off her sandals then kicking the denim and lace to the side.

I wasn't sure who was more frantic, me or her. She boldly stepped wide. Fuck, yes. She wasn't shy about her sexuality. She knew what she wanted, and that was my face between her thighs.

Good thing because that was exactly what I wanted too.

"You're going to come on my face, then you'll come on my dick."

"Promises, promises."

She was right. I wasn't doing this right if she was still talking. I wanted her to scream and forget her name. I was going to make that happen. My dick throbbed in my jeans, but it was staying in there until I got her off, or I'd have her on her back and be balls deep before she could say "condom."

While I loved my niece, I wasn't ready for kids of my own. Being in a fucking preschool was a good reminder that once it was time to fuck, we both needed to be protected. As she said, this was a fling. A wild fuck. Right?

Although the way I was feeling about Kelsey right now, once wasn't going to be enough. Not even close.

I was done warming her up. Done ensuring she was right here with me. She was going to come. Now. I got two fingers inside her and knew I found her G-spot when she cried out and rolled her hips. I rubbed that little spongy spot, pressed on it, and she jerked. Then I flicked her swollen clit with the tip of my tongue and learned the left side of that little pearl set her off. I curled and swirled, and she came. Her inner walls rippled, and her wetness coated my fingers. I felt like a fucking rock star. I'd satisfied this woman, pleasured her to the point where her knees buckled, and I had to use my free hand to grip her hip to keep her upright. Her eyes were closed, her chin tipped up toward the ceiling. And she was fucking silent.

She was stunning when she came. And I wanted to see that look again. I wanted to make her lose control. To give herself to me just like this. Not just this time.

Not just when I sank my dick inside her. Over and over for a long fucking time. I'd think about why that might be a problem later.

Yet the idea she'd walk away from me and some other guy would see her like this... I growled at the thought. No way anyone else could satisfy her like I could.

I pushed off the ground and picked her up as I did, carrying her over to the bed. It was fucking tiny, perhaps a twin or one of those narrow twins for a dorm room.

I was too big for that shit. I had been in college, and I was now. I set Kelsey on her feet, grabbed my wallet from my back pocket and dropped it on the made bed. Next, I undid my pants, pushed them down just enough so my cock sprang free. I sighed in relief. Kelsey sucked in a breath, which had me grinning as I sat on the side of the bed.

She stood before me, half naked. Her pussy with those fucking red curls was right in front of my face. I wanted to see her tits too, but I was too far gone. I had her taste in my mouth, her scent on my lips and chin. My balls were too full. She was that sexy.

I pulled a condom out. At the same time, Kelsey dropped to her knees and took me in her small hand although her fingers didn't make it all the way around.

My hips bucked.

I stilled, stared down at her. At her wild hair, her just-orgasmed look.

"Holy fuck," I murmured.

She was between my parted knees, dick in her grip. The crown was leaking pre-cum like a faucet and her warm breath fanned over it. As she leaned in and was about to get her mouth on it as if it were a fucking ice cream cone, I grabbed her by the arms and hoisted her up.

Her eyes widened in surprise, and she even looked disappointed. "What—"

"Shit, sugar, that's the hottest thing I've ever seen, but you get your mouth on me, and this is going to end before we get started."

She watched as I worked the condom on, then glanced up at her. "Climb on, sugar. Take me for a ride."

She studied me for a second, her breath coming in little excited pants. "You really are a cowboy."

"Should I say something about my big fire hose instead?"

Her nose crinkled. "Yeah, no." Her hands settled on my shoulders for balance as she set one knee on the bed beside my hip, then the other. I cupped her waist to steady her and help lift her. I grabbed my dick, and she shimmied until I was notched at her entrance.

My teeth clenched at the hot feel of her, even with only the head slipping inside.

"Oh fuck," I said as she worked herself down onto me.

I was big, but she was so fucking wet it was easy going.

Only when she was sitting on my thighs did she pause.

She met my gaze. Held.

Her inner walls clenched around me, and my balls drew up.

This woman. Holy fucking hell. She was incredible. Hot. Sweet. Wild. So fucking perfect.

She began to lift up, but her action was clumsy. She didn't have much traction on the narrow bed, so I took over, easily lifting and lowering her onto me.

Fucking her, thrusting my hips up every time I pulled her down.

I let go long enough to push her shirt up, and she grabbed it and took it off for me. I latched onto a nipple through the thin fabric of her bra then tugged down the lacy fabric of the cup to get to her bare skin.

I sucked on that pink tip as I gave over. I wasn't in

control any longer. My dick was. My need for this woman. It was so fierce. So... out of control.

"Kelsey," I murmured.

Our breathing was loud, the wet sounds of fucking filled the room. The slap of her thighs against mine. Her whimpers.

"You feel so fucking good," I whispered against her bouncing tit.

"Sawyer, oh my God."

Yup, my name and God. Job done.

Her inner walls began to milk and clench around me. She was close, and I grabbed her hip, rolled her forward to ensure her clit rubbed against me.

She came within seconds, thank fuck. While I was a generous lover and ensured she came first, not once but twice, I couldn't hold off any longer.

I was too far gone. My balls were aching to be emptied. My dick swelled, my fingers clenched on her hips. I thrust deep, held her still and spurted into the condom. Letting go and savoring the best orgasm of my life.

I wasn't sure how long I held her or how long my forehead rested between her tits. She wasn't saying a word.

I was so replete, so satisfied I wasn't done. This wasn't a quickie.

Well, it had been, so fucking hot and perfect. But I wasn't done with Kelsey. Not by a long shot, I realized in a moment of clarity, if I ever would be.

————

KELSEY

"Come to the ranch tomorrow. I want to see you again."

Sawyer's hand rested on my thigh. He'd set it there right after he turned his truck on and hadn't moved it since. We were just turning into the community center parking lot. Not much was said since... since he'd fucked me into silence.

I pointed to my car. It was the only one left in the lot.

I glanced at Sawyer, at the guy who'd just rocked my world. His hat was on the bench seat between us. The building's exterior lights were all that illuminated him, but I could see his short hair was tousled. All because of my fingers. I had to wonder if he had any bald patches because when he'd been eating me out, I'd yanked pretty hard.

Thankfully, he probably couldn't see the blush on

my cheeks just thinking about what we'd done. God, it had been hot. My pussy was a little sore from the workout. I'd come twice. *Twice.*

I was relaxed and sated. Content.

I barely knew the guy, and besides the fact he was skilled at annoying me—and making me come—I felt safe with him.

It was a little crazy. A little scary.

"Really?" I asked. "You don't have to. I mean, you're paying for your own date, so I'd say we're probably good."

He frowned, and his eyes narrowed. "I didn't fuck you as payment."

Oh shit. I stuck my foot in my mouth. He pulled his hand away, but I grabbed it. "I know. I didn't mean it that way. I mean... it was a fling. It's fine."

"No. That wasn't a fling. That was a warmup. I want that date you owe me."

"I *owe* you?" I released his hand, but it was his turn to grab me right back.

I laughed.

"A date, yeah." His thumb stroked over the inside of my wrist which shot little sparks of heat through my body. The way he looked at me indicated he was serious. He wanted to take me out.

"I don't like being beholden to a man," I admitted.

"Beholden? It's a date, sugar," he replied casually.

"It's just, the last guy did and said the same things."

"I'm not your ex."

"Fine." I gave in. I *wanted* to see him again. I wanted more of what we'd done in the preschool.

He leaned toward me, reached out and tucked my hair back. "Fine," he repeated, this time in a soft murmur, which threw me. We weren't arguing any more, and I wasn't exactly sure why we had in the first place. "Come to the ranch tomorrow. You can go for another ride."

I stared at him open mouthed, and he grinned.

"On a horse this time." He winked. "Then after, if you want to go all cowgirl on me again, I'm all for it. With a real bed though," he added.

He'd been pretty creative in the preschool's back room, so I wondered what Sawyer Manning could do to me if given some space and soft bedding.

"Okay," I whispered. I wanted to see him again. I did. I was just a little freaked because I felt something for him and not only in my pussy.

I'd told him this didn't mean anything. Well, it did, and that was the problem. A fling was one thing. Easy. Fun. No strings. This though, I'd somehow gotten myself all tangled up in a bunch of them without even trying. Shit.

"Tomorrow, then. I'll pick you up."

His words were like a bucket of ice water tossed on me. They cleared away the orgasm-induced fog and made reality return. Even though I was sleeping at the preschool, in the bed we'd just had sex on, he didn't know that. I wasn't going to tell him either. I couldn't. I wouldn't rely on someone like him, someone who seemed to be too good to be true. I'd learned the hard way they often were.

Sawyer Manning was a good guy. Sexy. Inventive. Attentive. A gentleman. Which meant I had to be careful. Really careful because it would be easy to fall for him. Heck, I was already a little bit in love with his dick.

"No," I said.

His eyes shifted from eager to guarded. "No?"

I blinked then gave him a rushed smile. "I mean, yes to tomorrow. You don't have to pick me up, though. I'll drive out," I replied.

His shoulders relaxed, and it made me feel good to see that he was relieved I'd said yes. He wanted this too.

"I had a good time tonight," I said. The cab of his truck was like a cocoon, a little bubble from the outside world. Once I opened the door, all my problems would return.

"Just good?" he asked, resting his forehead against mine. His big hand cupped the back of my neck. The heat of his touch seeped into me.

God, the feel of him, the strength. His... solidness made me want to climb back in his lap and just be.

I huffed out a little laugh. "Just good," I replied teasingly. This time without any of the heat or frustration I usually felt when he opened his mouth.

He growled then gave me a quick kiss. "Give me your cell before I show you better than good."

I blinked then pulled the device from my purse and handed it to him.

His thumbs slid over it, and I heard a beep coming from his shirt pocket. He handed the phone back. "I'll text you directions. Come after lunch."

I opened the door, looked over my shoulder at him. "Tomorrow," I said, as much as a goodbye as a promise.

He nodded.

I went to my car and climbed in. Looking in the rearview mirror, he hadn't left, and I realized he was waiting for me.

I started my car then pulled out of the spot and gave him a little wave. On the ride back to the preschool, I sank into thoughts of Sawyer Manning. His hands. His mouth. His hard body.

His diligence. I couldn't help the smile on my face.

I pulled into the parking spot behind the building Sawyer had used earlier and climbed from my car.

"Forget something?"

I stifled a scream and set my hand on my chest as I whipped my head around. There was Sawyer in his truck, window down. "Fudge, you scared me."

"I was following you home. Make sure you got there okay. Did you forget something?" he asked, tipping his head toward the building.

Oh shit. I couldn't tell him. I'd die inside if he knew. But he'd said he hated liars. "I... I—" I had to think of something and fast. "I forgot my paycheck. I wanted to get it, so I could deposit it at the bank in the morning."

He gave a little head nod of understanding.

"Thanks for following me, but I'm good from here. I'll see you tomorrow." I didn't wait for him to say anything more, only turned and opened the back door, gave him a little wave over my shoulder and went inside. I flipped the lock and leaned against the wall, the same place he'd kissed the hell out of me just a little while ago. I practically held my breath as I waited for him to pull away. He did a few seconds later.

I sighed and realized I was shaking. It was one

thing to keep the fact that I was living in the back room of the preschool a secret from Sarah Jane or anyone else in town. I'd be out of here soon enough, and it would be as if it hadn't happened. I'd thought it would be no big deal with Sawyer as well. But after a few hours together, he'd made me feel things. *New* things I couldn't grasp, but I liked. A lot. I wanted to see him on his ranch tomorrow. I wanted to be with him. To get to know him and not just naked. He hadn't even gotten naked earlier, and now that I thought about it, what a total shame.

I don't like liars, Sawyer had said.

Dread settled in my stomach. I'd just lied to him. Not about something small but a big deal. I'd fallen for Tom, the married asshole. While Tom had nothing to do with the shitty, thieving roommate I'd found, I was still paying the price for following him to Montana. I'd spent my entire life trying to be nothing like my mother and then, without even realizing it, had done the same stupid things as her. Walked away from a life in Colorado—an apartment, a job—for a man. Then fell flat on my face. Gah!

I went to the cabinet and grabbed my toiletry bag, took it into the bathroom with the pint-sized toilet and sink. Bending at the waist, I looked at myself in the mirror. I brushed my fingertips over a little red mark on my neck and remembered the feel of his lips. It wasn't an all- out hickey, but he'd marked me. My pussy clenched at how in control he'd been. How he'd actually gotten me to forget everything but his name.

Was I falling for the sex? Was I just like my mother with Sawyer, falling into bed without even going on a date? I could have sex, a one-night stand, and have it not be more than that. Except I wanted *more than that.* It was the fact that I wanted to go back for more that had me worried.

Sawyer was a great guy. God, a *really* great guy. Was I thinking that because I was desperate? I couldn't let someone big and strong rescue me because I couldn't become reliant. I couldn't expect a guy to be there for me, to take care of me in the *right* way.

He was nothing like Tom. Nothing like the string of men my mother had hooked onto. But if I relied on Sawyer Manning, I'd be nothing different than my mother, proving I couldn't stand on my own two feet.

I laughed at myself in the kiddie mirror. I was doing a shit job of that.

6

ELSEY

I MIGHT HAVE BEEN hard on myself the night before and questioned whether I should even go to Sawyer's ranch, but when I'd discovered that he'd texted me when I'd been in the shower at the community center, I'd felt like a high school girl with her first crush.

I hadn't been able to help the sappy smile that had spread across my face as I'd gotten dressed. Or the way my nipples hardened at the thought of being with him again. I'd ignored every doubting thought in my head, maybe even some of the smarter ones. I hadn't been able to say no to his invitation. I *wanted* to be with him.

He'd sent directions since he'd said it was too far out of town for any map on my phone to be accurate. As I parked in front of the beautiful ranch house and climbed from my car, I realized there was more to Sawyer Manning than just a sexy smile. Irene had said the Manning boys were all rich and gorgeous. I'd only met Sawyer, and I agreed with her on his looks. The pickup he drove hadn't given off any indication that he was wealthy. It was at least thirty years old without any features like power windows or heated seats even though it was kept in pristine, restored condition.

This house though. It wasn't flashy or a mansion like some down near the ski resort. But it was big, and it had clearly been here awhile. I looked around, took in the killer views, the prairie that went on and on. Only a few buildings dotted the land, but I had a feeling they were part of the Manning ranch not neighbors. There was money here. I just couldn't imagine why Delilah, with her high heels and designer jeans, would want to live all the way out here. The nearest sidewalk was ten miles away. But I shouldn't have been all that surprised because my mother had been driven by money enough to live on a yacht for three months with Guy Number Four when she got seasick looking at a waterbed.

"Hello, Kelsey."

I spun around at a woman's voice. She stood on the porch, wiping her hands on an apron. "Miss Alice. Hi there."

"Duck!" The deep voice came from behind her. A man appeared with Claire on his shoulders. She leaned down, so they could fit through the doorway.

"Kelsey!" the little girl squealed then wiggled enough for the man to put her on her feet. She ran down the steps and hugged my leg.

I couldn't help but smile at her exuberance.

"Easy, sprout. Don't knock her off her feet."

This had to be one of Sawyer's brothers although the only similarity was their size. This guy had fair hair and a narrower face. He was sporting jeans and a police uniform shirt. He had a gun at his hip.

"I'm Huck Manning. You clearly know Claire." When he met my gaze, I realized he had the same eyes as Sawyer.

I stroked the girl's blonde hair and nodded to the guy.

"Heard you bought my brother last night." He grinned, and I could see why Irene thought the Manning brothers were *all* gorgeous. If I hadn't met

Sawyer, I'd have fallen for Huck. But I hadn't. Huck was hot. No question, but there was something about Sawyer that did it for me.

I couldn't help the blush, and I glanced down at Claire.

"Why didn't you buy Daddy instead?" she asked, looking up at me with a sweet earnestness.

"Claire," Alice said.

She turned to look at Alice, and her little ringlets bounced. "What? She'd make a good mommy."

Huck ran a hand over the back of his neck in obvious embarrassment, and Alice sucked in a breath.

I was used to kids without filters, and I couldn't help but laugh.

"Claire Manning," Alice whispered although Claire didn't seem the least bit contrite. I had a feeling she really did want a mother.

"Besides, I think Seesaw would have a problem with that," Huck said, coming down to join us. While he was smiling, he gave me a quick, contrite glance before grabbing Claire and tossing her over his shoulder. Fireman style, just like Sawyer had done with me the night before. She giggled and wiggled as he carried her back to the porch and set her back on her feet in front of him, his hands on her shoulders, so she wouldn't run off again.

Footsteps came from behind me. "What would I have a problem with?"

I didn't have to turn to know it was Sawyer. My nipples had gone instantly hard at the voice. When I turned, he was walking my way, grinning. He looked good in jeans and a blue shirt that matched the color of his eyes. His hat was tugged low, and the way he was looking at me... at my chest, I knew my shirt wasn't hiding my response.

"Hi, Seesaw!" Claire called.

"You can't have Kelsey," Sawyer said to Claire, slipping an arm around my shoulders. "Seesaw wants her. Your daddy got bought last night, too."

Claire froze, her eyes widened, and her mouth dropped open. Slowly, she turned around to look up at him. "You did? Will she be my mommy?"

"Working on it, sprout." He steered her back into the house and offered a little wave over his shoulder as they disappeared inside. I wasn't sure what that meant, but it didn't seem like we'd find out right now.

Alice gave me another smile and nod. "It was good to see you."

"Same," I replied, then she turned and followed the others back into the house.

Sawyer turned and tipped my chin up with a finger. His eyes roved over my face and settled on my lips. Then he kissed me. Gentle and quick. Goose-bumps rose on my arms even though it was eighty degrees out.

"Seesaw?" I asked when he lifted his head.

"Claire couldn't say Sawyer, and it's stuck. Come on."

He took my hand and steered me away from the house and down a dirt drive. "Where are we going?"

"My place."

I frowned and looked around. His truck wasn't here. "Did I go to the wrong place?"

"Doesn't matter." He tipped his chin and pointed in front of us. "That was the big house where I grew up. Huck and Claire live there now with Alice."

"Your mom?" I glanced up at him as we walked side by side.

He squeezed my fingers, and I felt the callouses made from hard work. "No, our parents have been gone for a long time now."

"I'm... I'm sorry to hear that." I couldn't imagine what had happened to them, but he and his brothers must have been young.

He gave me a small smile in response. "Alice calls herself the Manning housekeeper although she's so much more than that. She's been here since before I was born."

I'd met the woman a number of times at the preschool's drop off and pickup. I'd always assumed she was Claire's grandmother. One thing I'd done with the Mannings was make lots of assumptions. Hopefully, this time with Sawyer would fix that.

We got to the top of a slight rise, and his house came into view. It wasn't as large as the "big house," but it was made of log and river rock, a two-car garage off to the side. It had a porch that wrapped around three sides, all with amazing views. It was beautiful and impressive. Just like the guy who'd built it.

"Wow. It's really great, Sawyer," I said.

He stared at his home with an odd look. Satisfaction, perhaps. Pride, definitely. Both were understandable. "I started building it during college, coming home for the summers and working on it."

"You built this?" I asked, staring in awe. There was a lot to this guy. Hardworking. Cared for his family. A civil servant for his community.

He shrugged as if it was no big deal to build a *house*. "I had help. When I graduated, I moved back, started working for the fire department. Never left."

"You didn't want to stay in the one house together?"

"My great-great-granddaddy built a homestead

here." He waved his hand out to the vast land in front of us. "Manning land is all you see."

I didn't think he said that to be boastful, but to point out why he lived here. Why it was important to him.

"The oldest part of the big house is what he built. Then generations since have added on. I've always known I'd live on this land. But I needed a place of my own. Something mine. Thatcher, who you haven't met, converted the original barn." He pointed to the left and to a white building in the distance. I couldn't imagine a close family like his, who wanted to be near each other, to live on the land that had belonged to their family for decades and for future generations. The view was spectacular but empty.

"This is a long way from the fire station. What if there's a fire?"

"The department's a mix of paid and volunteer firefighters. As chief, I'm paid, so I work a consistent schedule. I fight fires, but I also deal with administration. The annoying paperwork. I'm on call sometimes and stay at the station then, but otherwise, like now, I'm off."

———

SAWYER

I HAD no idea why Kelsey's reaction to seeing the ranch was vital. I'd been eager to see her. So had my dick. Every time I thought of her, I got hard. Which meant I'd been able to pound nails with my dick since I left her the night before. I couldn't get the way she'd gone all soft and... fuck, perfect in my arms. I had no idea why it was different with her. Fate. Kismet. Destiny. Any of those woowoo words. I didn't give a shit what it was labeled, but I wanted Kelsey.

I didn't bring women to the ranch. I'd learned my lesson with Tina. I didn't want any woman to want the Manning property more than me. I wanted the woman I'd marry to fall in love with the land. That was important because I sure as shit wasn't moving, and she would help shape the property's future. Give me the kids that would take over from me and my brothers.

Yet I hadn't been into any woman enough since Tina to even consider having her come to the ranch. I fucked. I wasn't a monk but never here. I dated, but again, not here. That was why Alice had volunteered me for the bachelor auction. I hadn't brought a woman around. Not one I was serious about.

Until now.

I hadn't even thought about it the night before when I'd invited Kelsey. The words had been said before I even thought about it. I'd meant them. Hadn't wanted to take them back.

Seeing Kelsey in front of the big house with Claire hugging her, it made me think of more than just making Kelsey mine. For the first time in my life, I thought of ditching the condoms and getting her pregnant, seeing her round with a child we made. I pictured a beautiful redheaded little girl running around although only after we made a few boys to watch out for her first.

Was I crazy? Fuck, yes, because I'd only thought of kids as something down the road. Even the night before in the preschool. No longer. I was ready now. Huck and Thatcher would think I was pussy whipped. I didn't give a shit.

I steered her away from my house, not letting go of her hand, and toward the stable.

She looked over her shoulder. "Aren't you going to give me a tour?"

"If we go inside, the only tour you're going to get is of my bed, so I thought it safer to stay away."

I was strong willed but not where she was concerned, especially if she took off her clothes.

She slowed, and I shortened my long gait to keep

pace. She looked up at me through those red lashes, her cheeks pink. "Safer?"

I took in her jeans and sleeveless top. Sneakers. The hint of makeup on her face. That red tangle of hair pulled back into a ponytail. Her outfit wasn't the least bit alluring. There wasn't a hint of cleavage showing. Only her arms were bare. But since I knew what she looked like naked, she could wear a cloth sack, and I'd find her sexy as hell.

My dick was uncomfortably hard, and I had to adjust myself. Her gaze dropped to the action. "Yeah, safer," I said, not needing to offer any other explanation. "Come on, I want to show you something in the stable."

Something where I wouldn't want to rip the clothes from her body and bend her over a bale of hay.

Fuck, now I was thinking about that. There was no place I didn't want another round with her.

"Is it something I'm going to want to ride?"

I practically skidded to a stop, turned and glared at her. An impish smile turned her lips. "Sugar, I know I mentioned that last night, but I'm trying to be a gentleman. Be a good girl."

She looked me over from head to toe, her perusal anything but ladylike.

I growled and tugged her further away from the house. My bed. Her soft laugh had me smiling.

The interior of the stable was cool, the tang of horses and manure was strong, but with the great weather, the doors were open.

"I've never ridden a horse," she admitted, as I went up to a dappled mare who stuck her head out of her stall.

I rubbed her nose. "You can touch her," I said.

When she didn't reach out, I took her hand in mine and started to raise it. I felt her tense the closer we got. "Sugar, she's not going to hurt you."

Her eyes widened, and she actually looked afraid. "This is Sable. She's gentle. Claire rides her."

She laughed then. "Claire's braver than me."

"Nah, she's just been around them. I'll get you liking them in no time. For now, just give her a pat."

I waited for her to take a deep breath then nod. I raised her hand and set it on Sable's neck then let go. Just stood there and watched as she stroked her, her eyes wide, and the smile on her face genuine.

I went to grab some oats from a bucket and came back, held my palm out for Sable to eat. "Wanna try?"

She dropped her hand, wiped it on her jeans and eyed Sable as if she were an alligator instead of a docile mare. "No way. Those teeth are huge."

I grinned. "Another time."

"She's what you want to show me?"

"Down here." I set my hand on the small of her back and guided her down to the stall at the end. She looked inside and gasped.

"Puppies!"

I opened the stall door, and she went in and knelt down. "That's Maple," I said, introducing Kelsey to the yellow Lab. "She's Thatcher's." The dog raised her head but didn't move as seven squiggly Labrador puppies nursed from her. One got bumped out of the way, and Kelsey picked the guy up and hugged him to her for a moment before she set him back in place to keep eating.

"Aren't you a pretty mommy?" Kelsey crooned as she pet Maple then looked up at me. "You're good."

I leaned against the stall, crossed my ankles. "Oh?"

She narrowed her eyes. "Puppies? Seriously?"

I tilted my hat. I couldn't help but be amused at her look. "What?"

She cocked her head and rolled her eyes. "Don't 'what' me. Are you trying to win me over with puppies?"

I looked down the length of the stable, ensured we were alone before I spoke. "I was thinking I'd won you over with my dick."

She blushed and got to her feet. Came over to me. She was smiling. At me.

"Puppies and a magical dick. What more could a girl want?"

Going up on her toes, she hooked her hand behind my neck and pulled me down for a kiss.

I instantly took over, wrapping my hands around her, one hand cupping her perfect ass and lifting her. She wrapped her legs around me, and I turned, pressing her into the wall, just like the night before. She was so soft and curvy, my hands able to get a grip on her and hold on.

I hadn't anticipated kissing her now, rolling my hips against her center and making her moan. But I wasn't going to turn the opportunity down.

She lifted her head an inch or so to catch her breath. "You sure know how to make a girl hot."

"Your panties get wet for puppies, sugar?"

She shook her head and grinned. "My panties get wet for the guy who has puppies."

And that was it. Right there. Boom. My restraint was gone. My need for this woman pushed me past being a gentleman. Past waiting to get her in my bed to have her again.

I pushed up her shirt, baring her lace covered breasts, bent down and took one pink nipple into my mouth. Her back arched and her hands settled on my head. It wasn't close enough, so I tugged down the cup to bare her to me. "Fucking gorgeous," I breathed then took her back in my mouth.

"We're in the stable," she said.

"No one will come in," I said although I couldn't be completely sure of that.

"I thought you wanted to wait," she breathed.

I kissed across the swell of her tits to the other one. "Can't wait. Need to get in what's mine."

Carefully, I lowered her legs back to the ground, so I could undo the button on her jeans and slide the zipper down.

"Sawyer, I can't be—"

With room now, I slid my hand into the front of her panties, and she went up onto her toes when I slid one finger deep into her dripping pussy. Fuck, yes. So tight. So hot. Her walls were rippling around my finger, and if the night before was any indication, she was close to coming. "What, sugar?"

"Don't stop." Her hands went to my wrist, guiding me as she wanted, her hips rolling.

I grinned and watched her face as she fucked herself on my finger. When she went over the edge, crying out my name in the stable, I almost came in my jeans.

With a hand on her hip to steady her, I pulled the other from her panties, licked my finger clean. I'd never get enough of the sweet taste of her pussy.

Her lips were parted, and she slowly opened her eyes. Then she went at me, frantic. Her hands were suddenly on my jeans and getting them open. Fuck, yes.

Somehow, I had enough blood left in my brain to realize something.

I stilled her hand. "Sugar, I don't have a condom."

She tipped her head up and blinked.

"We have to go to my house."

She shook her head, breathing hard. "Too far away."

Fuck. *Fuck.*

It was my turn to grab her wrist. To keep her from pulling my dick out. Of course, if she got her hand on it right now, it'd be all over. No condom needed. I let out a deep breath. "I'm game for knocking you up but not yet. Maybe get a ring on your finger first."

She blinked up at me.

"Your pussy greedy and needing more? I'll eat you out, sugar."

I moved away from her, grabbed a horse blanket from a hook on the wall and dropped it onto the straw away from the dogs. I sat down, knees bent and curled my finger.

She came over and knelt beside me. "Your turn." Her hands went back to my jeans, got them open, and I lifted my hips to push them down below my ass along with my boxers. My dick sprang free, and I sighed in relief then hissed when she gripped me firmly at the base and stroked up the entire length.

I fell back on my elbows and watched as she lowered her head, opened those plump lips and took me deep.

"Holy fuck." My eyes fell closed as I set my hand on the back of her head, careful not to push down and make her take too much. She was doing a killer job without any guidance from me.

Her hair was a fiery tangle around her, strands of it tickling my bare lower belly. Her jeans were open, and I could now see her panties were pale blue, the same color as her bra.

My balls were tight, and the suction of her mouth was making me lose my mind.

I dropped onto my back. "Climb on my face, sugar. I want that pussy while you suck me dry."

She lifted her head, licked her swollen lips as she looked at me. The cool air on my wet dick wasn't easing my need at all.

I crooked my finger again, and then she smiled, pushing her jeans and panties down, then swung her leg over my chest. I grasped her hip and pulled her back toward my face and—

Fuck me.

Pink pussy. Hard little clit. Red curls. *Right there.*

I licked my lips and pulled her down, so I got my mouth on her.

She cried out. "Sawyer. I... slow down."

I liked a woman who gave her man directions. I did as told and was rewarded when she shifted and licked up the length of me from root to tip. When she gripped me again—her other hand propping her up over me—and took me deep, I almost couldn't focus. *Almost.* My goal now was to get her off before I came down her throat. I licked, sucked, even got my fingers into it, finding her G-spot and making her ride my face. She may never have been on a horse, but she sure as shit knew how to ride.

She came again, her knees squeezing my shoulders. Her sweet honey dripped onto my fingers, my tongue. I lasted all of five seconds after she buried her pussy on my face, my cum pumping down her throat. She swallowed me down. Every bit.

I tipped her to the side, and she slumped onto the blanket beside me, her head resting on my stomach. A smile curled her lips, and she looked up at me in a way I wanted to see on her face every fucking day.

"I want to see Sandy!"

Claire's voice had me closing my eyes and groaning and Kelsey popping up faster than a piece of bread from a toaster. "No one will come in?" she hissed.

Thankfully, we only had to get our jeans fixed. Kelsey spun around in a circle, then dropped to her knees beside Maple before Claire tore into the stall. "Did you see my new puppy?"

The smile on Kelsey's face was for Claire, but I knew the flush to her cheeks was my doing. And those swollen lips... fuck, I was getting hard again.

Thatcher stopped just inside the stall. He glanced from Kelsey to me where I still sat on the blanket. He arched a brow and grinned. Yeah, he knew what we'd been up to, at least the general idea. Fortunately, Claire didn't see anything but wriggling puppies.

"You're keeping one?"

"Yes, and I've named her Sandy."

"Which one?" Kelsey asked, wiping her lips with her fingers.

Claire tipped her head just like Huck did and studied the line of little sand colored bodies, too small to be told apart, then turned to look up at Thatcher. "Which one's Sandy?"

"Claire Bear, think you want to be a little lady and introduce me to your friend?" Thatcher asked.

Claire giggled. "Uncle Thatch, this is Miss Kelsey, my teacher."

Thatcher took off his Stetson and leaned toward Kelsey and shook her hand. "Your teacher or Seesaw's friend?"

Claire looked to me with the same pale blue eyes as her daddy. And me and Thatcher. She was definitely a Manning. "She bought Seesaw, so she's going to keep him."

Kelsey turned as red as her hair. "Which one's Sandy?" she asked, clearly redirecting Claire, which worked because she spun about and stared with a scrunched-up face trying to tell the difference between the furry balls.

Thatcher squatted down behind Claire and set his hand on her little shoulder, her focus completely on the dogs. "Nice to meet you, Kelsey. I'll let you get back to testing out your purchase."

Kelsey's mouth dropped open, and he winked at her. I stood, went over to him and whacked him on the back of the head.

He raised his shoulders and scrunched down in

defense, but his grin showed he was completely unrepentant.

"Time to go, sugar."

I held out my hand and helped Kelsey to her feet. "It's time for the house tour."

"Have fun you two," Thatcher called.

We sure as shit would.

 ELSEY

I WAS in big trouble here. Hot guy. *Nice* guy. Great family. Puppies. Magical dick. I couldn't figure out what was wrong with Sawyer Manning besides the fact that I wanted him *too* much. This couldn't be right. It was lust. It was infatuation. It was fleeting.

But it felt so good. Giddy. Light. Flirty. Sexy.

Sawyer wasn't hiding anything. Not like Tom who'd kept all his secrets in a different state. He was showing me everything, every facet of him as if the truth was important.

He... and the puppies were impossible to resist.

Especially when he kissed me like he needed it to survive. Talked dirty to me as if he was far from a gentleman. As he walked me through his house, I realized I was out of my league. The place wasn't fancy, but it was obvious he had money. He drove an eighties pickup truck around. He didn't flash his cash. But the granite countertops, the high-end appliances, floor to ceiling windows, the supersized shower with more jets than an airplane all showed that he hadn't skimped. The walls were a soft tan, area rugs covered the hardwood floors. Decorations were kept to a minimum and were neutral and masculine. I loved it. It felt like... home. When he showed me the three bedrooms, two of them empty, I remembered what he'd said in the heat of the moment.

I'm game for knocking you up but not yet. Maybe get a ring on your finger first.

My heart flipped over, and I had a little flash of panic. He wanted kids. With me. He wanted to put a ring on it. *On me.*

Everything I owned fit in the tiny storage unit and my car. I was sleeping in the back room of my work. I had no savings. Nothing.

And yet when he leaned down and kissed my shoulder as he stood behind me and I stared at his huge bed in the master bedroom, I couldn't help but tilt my head to the side.

"What's the matter?" he asked, his warm breath fanning my neck.

"There aren't any curtains," I said, staring at the huge windows, which were open to let in the summer air.

I felt his lips turn up in a smile. "The lack of curtains bothers you?"

I gave a slight shrug and bumped his mouth. "Don't you like it dark to sleep?"

"I'm an early riser."

"What about people seeing you... I mean, in your underwear or something."

"There's no one around to see."

"You have brothers," I countered.

"Trust me, they don't want to see me in my underwear. You're not checking out the big bed?"

"It's a beautiful quilt," I commented.

Sawyer was neat. His bed was made. No clothes were strewn across the floor. Only his firefighter uniform shirt was out, but it was folded and laying over an armchair in the corner, positioned directly next to a now-cold fireplace. I could only imagine how cozy that spot would be to read in the dead of winter.

"My mother made it. It was on my parents' bed."

I turned just enough to look up at him. "What happened to them?"

"Small plane crash. My father was a pilot, and his little Cessna hit a wind shear."

I couldn't imagine losing both parents at the same time. Not a mom and dad like what I thought his would be like. Loving. Open. Devoted, not only to each other but their kids.

"How old were you?"

"Fifteen. You said your mom was in Phoenix?"

I closed my eyes and rested my head against his shoulder. Sighed. "Yeah. She goes through men like most people go through underwear."

"That fast?"

"Okay, maybe as fast as most people replace their furnace filter. Better?"

"I'm getting a much better picture now. Thanks."

I couldn't help but smile. I reached back and tried to pinch his side, but it was all hard muscle. I was equally annoyed and turned on.

"Are you close?"

"Only when she needs money. I never knew my dad."

"Brothers and sisters?"

"Nope."

"I'm sorry, sugar. That must be hard with your mom. I can't imagine not relying on my family, even if they are sometimes a pain in the ass."

"I'm used to it. I can take care of myself," I reiterated, perhaps as much for him as for me.

"You might have taken care of your orgasms before, sugar. It's my job now. So, the bed..." he murmured, his lips now on my neck. His cell rang, and he stepped back and pulled it from his pocket.

"Manning." He turned away from me, walked over to the window and stared out as he listened.

My head was still spinning with his last words. It was his job to take care of my orgasms? Um... what? He'd given me a handful in the short time I'd known him. They were so much better than any I'd ever given myself, either with my hand or a vibrator. I was equally thrilled and bothered by his possessiveness.

He glanced over his shoulder at me. Sighed. "Fine. I'll be there as soon as I can."

He hung up, shoved the device back in his pocket.

"Sorry, sugar. That was the station. There's an issue with the fire truck. A part was shipped, but it was the wrong one. Someone's headed to Helena to get a replacement, but... well, the reason doesn't matter. I have to go."

"I understand."

He came over to me, tucked my hair back. His blue eyes moved between mine, dipped to my mouth. "Raincheck on my bed? I've got plans for you, and they might take a while. Might have to keep you naked and too satisfied to leave."

When he took my hand and walked me back to my car, I was equally thrilled and freaked. I wanted to be with Sawyer, but he was talking babies and rings and *keeping* me. We barely knew each other, and that meant the luster would wear off. My pussy wouldn't be that special any longer, and he'd be ready to move on. And then what?

————

SAWYER

MAYBE IT WAS THE ORGASMS. Maybe it was Kelsey's smile. Maybe it was the way she fit so perfectly in my arms. Maybe it was the way she rode my face while she sucked me off so perfectly. Or maybe I was just whipped. Kelsey was it for me. There was something about her, maybe the fact that she wasn't all sweet and timid. Hell no. She'd gotten down in the hay and gone wild.

She wanted to be independent. Didn't want to rely on a guy. I could understand that, especially after what she told me of her ex.

But it was in my DNA to take care of a woman. I'd thought that was what Tina had wanted, a man to watch out for her and protect her. But she'd wanted the protection of the Manning money not me.

I never expected to find Kelsey. Never knew it would be like this. I fell for her. Hard. Fast.

She was sweet with Claire and wild with me.

Uninhibited one moment, cautious the next. I knew I could get past those walls she had solidly built. Every time I got her to stop thinking, I saw the real Kelsey. The one I hoped would want me right back.

She was caring. Sexy. Prickly. Fun. Wild. *My* woman. Yeah, I was fucking keeping her and not just because she was a dirty girl in the hay.

I just had to figure out how to tell her. I could show her over and over until she believed my actions. I'd hoped to do just that, spending the day in my bed. I'd hinted that I wanted more, wanted long term with her, but had not said it outright. I'd tell her the words when I felt confident, and I wouldn't be kneed in the nuts.

As I followed her back into town, I realized I had no idea where she lived. Another thing I needed to figure out because I planned to spend every night I could with her, and if she lived downtown, it would be a hell of a lot closer to the station than the ranch.

She signaled for the community center, and I turned in behind her. The fire station was three blocks down. Since I had a few minutes, I pulled up beside her car. She was reaching into the back seat and grabbing a bag when I said, "Funny seeing you here."

My window was down, and my elbow rested in the opening. The sun was warm on my skin.

She spun around, shoving the bag back in the car, her hair whipping into her face. I knew why it was all wild and tangled, and I couldn't help the caveman feelings knowing it was from sixty-nine. My new favorite position although I was headed to the convenience store after this for the largest box of condoms they sold.

"Are you... are you following me?" she asked, her gaze darting around.

My smile slipped as she didn't look all that happy to see me. I pointed out the front windshield. "The station's just down the road. I thought I'd get one more kiss before—"

"Sawyer, I don't like you following me."

I looked to the community center, trying to figure out why she was so bent out of shape.

"You seem awful cranky for someone who came all over my face just a little while ago. You need some more lovin'?"

Her cheeks turned pink as I'd hoped, but instead of seeing desire in her eyes, they narrowed.

I put the truck in park and held up my hands. "Whoa, sugar. That look might fell a lesser man."

"Sawyer," she said, and not in that hot, breathy way she did earlier.."

I rubbed the back of my neck. "I'm not sure what happened between the ranch and here, but I've got to deal with the bad part at the station, and then I can come to your place. Talk through whatever's bothering you. Lend an ear."

She shook her head, tucked her hair back behind her ear. "No. God, look, this has been fun. I'm sorry, but I can't do this."

I frowned. "Do what?"

"I can't *stay in your bed for a long time*." Her hands came up, and she made those annoying air quotes. "I can't be what you want."

Whatever happiness I felt just a minute ago was fading away. Now I was fucking confused. Pissed. The more she got wound up, the calmer I became. "What is it you think I want, sugar?"

"It was supposed to be just sex. I *told* you this didn't mean anything."

"What's happened? What's got you this way in the twenty minutes from the ranch? Someone call you?"

Her cheeks flared with color, and she glanced away. Yeah, someone had bothered her. Someone had got thoughts in her head.

"Who's bothered you? Let me help you."

"No!" she cried.

A mother carrying a toddler glanced our way as she went to her car. I gave her a little wave with my hand that rested on the steering wheel.

Kelsey stepped up to my car window, looked me in the eye. "I don't need your help, Sawyer Manning. I was doing just fine on my own before you showed up."

"You bought me at the auction, if you remember," I reminded her.

"I'll get you your money."

I looked up at the ceiling in my truck and gritted my teeth. "I don't give a shit about the money. I give a shit about *you*."

"No. No!" she repeated, stepping back, hands in front of her. "I'll get you the money. Until then, leave me alone." She turned away.

"Wait," I said, climbing from my truck. I reached out to touch her but changed my mind at the last second. "That's it? After what we just did?"

"It was sex. Sex!" She tossed her arms up in the air although the way she was acting, I could tell she thought the complete opposite. "I can't fall for a guy just because he's got a magic dick."

I was pleased she thought my dick was magical, but I was pissed more. "I thought you liked me for more than my dick. I mean, at least the puppies."

That got a small smile out of her as she ran a hand through her hair. Tugged, looked everywhere but at me. "I... I can't."

"Who got you all riled up? Your momma? Someone else?"

She ignored my questions and looked away. I didn't miss the tears in her eyes. Someone had hurt her, and instead of coming to me, she was pushing me away. "It's better this way."

I stood there, hands on hips, and watched as she grabbed her bag from the back seat, slammed her door and ran for the building.

What the fuck had just happened?

———

KELSEY

I MADE it all the way to the ladies' locker room and into a bathroom stall before I lost it. God, Sawyer had looked... bewildered. Frustrated. Angry, even.

My mother had texted me earlier when I'd been at the ranch. I'd left my cell in my car, and I'd missed the note until I'd pulled up to a red light, and I'd checked my phone.

Mom: *Roger broke up with me. I need money for rent.*

I ASSUMED Roger was Mr. Phoenix, but I couldn't be sure, just another long string of guys who'd let my mother down. If the pattern held, she'd fallen for Roger, moved into his place then got tossed aside when he was bored with her.

She had no degree. No skills. She'd barely held a job. Her *job* had been to find a sugar daddy to take care of her and me when I'd been little. But now she was *fired from her job* and was broke.

It had hit way too close to home for me. I might have gone to college and had a job, but I'd followed

Tom to a new state. I'd thought I loved him. But the way I felt for Sawyer was so much more, and I'd only known him a day. It had been only last night when I'd bought him at the auction.

Last night!

I'd *told* him this didn't mean anything. I'd meant it. But somewhere between ice cream and puppies, I'd gone from wanting meaningless sex with him to... everything?

In. A. Day.

I was *just* like my mother. Thank God she'd texted. Serendipitous, in fact. I hadn't heard from her in months, and her text had been the reminder I needed.

I was turning into her. I couldn't rely on a man.

Not Sawyer Manning.

Especially not him. I'd gone to the community center to shower, and he'd followed me. If I hadn't been so freaked that he'd find out what I was up to, I'd have found it endearing.

He'd wanted a kiss.

A kiss.

Tears filled my eyes because he must think I am crazy or had the worst case of PMS ever.

He was so close to finding out I had no place to live. When he learned the truth, he'd be pissed that I'd lied to him. Or worse, he'd help me.

I couldn't let him do that. If I did, I'd be stepping right into my mother's footsteps. I'd be reliant on him. I had to stand on my own. To take care of myself.

Guys don't stick. They have their fun, and when they get bored, they move on. Or they lie like Tom to have their fun with no intention of more.

So I pushed Sawyer away. The guy who made me feel. To make me hope.

I swiped at the tears that slid down my cheeks, grabbed some toilet paper and wiped my face. It was better this way.

As I grabbed my things and headed to the showers, I had to wonder why.

8

 ELSEY

THE SHATTER of glass woke me. I hadn't realized I'd fallen asleep because I'd tossed and turned for hours. All I could think about was Sawyer. The look on his face when I'd pushed him away. The desire to grab my phone and call him. Pick up my keys and drive to his house and make things right.

I wanted him. Needed him in a way that scared me, and that was why I hadn't done anything. I'd stayed on the cot and willed myself to sleep. It must have worked until now.

I popped up in bed, listened. There was someone

outside the building. I climbed from the bed, went to the window and looked out. I didn't see anything but the back parking lot. Then I smelled it. Gasoline. I dashed into the main room of the school and froze. Fire. It was spreading up the wall by the sharing corner, the children's finger paintings on the wall curling up and burning. The preschool had originally been a miner's house from the turn of the century. The turn of the *last* century. I didn't know the building's history or how long it had been a school, but it didn't have sprinklers. It was made of wood. The walls, the shingles on the roof. The floors. Everything. There were fire extinguishers in every room and fire code requirements like exit signs, but the flames were spreading too fast for me to put out. I was in a tank top and sleep shorts, and I could feel the heat from the flames touching my skin.

I coughed, ran back to my bed and grabbed my cell from the floor. The shattered window had the fire pulling toward it, the glass coating the alphabet carpet.

A whoosh came from outside, and I ran to the front window. A man was pouring liquid on the building. Lifting and swinging, the... oh shit, gas was splashing off the wall. He stepped back, dropped the can. He was in shadow, and I couldn't make out his face or anything more than that he was wearing a dark hoodie and dark pants. He lit a match and tossed it. The flames erupted, and he didn't linger, turning and running for a car at the curb. He sped off, the engine revving hard.

I coughed, the smoke starting to fill the room. I went to the back door, flipped the lock and ran out. I had no idea if the guy would come to the back, but I wasn't waiting around to find out. If he would set a building on fire, he was dangerous enough to do something else. Like hurt me, the one person who'd watched his crime.

I dashed for the trees on the far side of the parking lot and hid behind a huge cottonwood. Leaning against the rough bark, I fumbled with my phone. I was too panicked, too keyed up to type in my unlock code, so I pushed the Emergency button. I'd never appreciated such a feature before now.

"9-1-1, what is your emergency?"

"A fire. The preschool on South Grant is on fire."

———

SAWYER

. . .

AFTER REPLACING the bad part on the engine, I'd stayed at the station, hanging with the guys instead of going home. While she hadn't been in my bed yet, going home was going to remind me of the fun afternoon we'd had. I doubted I'd be able to go into the stable ever again without getting hard. Anything to avoid thinking about whatever the fuck happened at the community center earlier.

When the call came in for a structure fire, I'd been with the others to get the firetruck rolling in under two minutes. We were able to see the glow of the flames as soon as we left the bay. By the time we pulled up, got the hoses laid and the water on the preschool, the front was fully engulfed. Fortunately, there was enough land around it that no other buildings downtown were threatened. It didn't take long to push down the flames, but my crew would be handling hot spots longer.

Neighbors had come out to watch, but they'd stayed back. I finished rolling up one of the hose lines and caught sight of Huck. Tipped my chin in greeting. I expected to see him here at some point. Our jobs overlapped often. The street was blocked off, and he cut across it to join me. Flashing blue lights from all the emergency vehicles bounced off his grim features.

I shrugged off my heavy fire jacket, so I was just in

my bunker pants. Sweat made my t-shirt cling, but the night air felt good. "Sometimes I hate my job," I muttered.

Huck grunted. "Place went up fast," he commented.

"Too fast," I replied.

"Accelerant?"

I nodded. "The scent of it is strong close to the building. Not all of it burned off."

His jaw clenched. A house fire was one thing, but arson in The Bend?

I ran a hand over my face. "At least there weren't any kids in there."

Huck's eyes narrowed, and he looked up at the black sky and took a breath. This was Claire's school, and the idea of her and any of the other kids being inside...

Fuck.

A woman in sweats and slippers came over to us. Forty, maybe, although it was hard to tell in the harsh lights and at midnight. No one looked all that great pulled from their bed. She set one hand on her chest as she tried to catch her breath.

"I'm Irene. I run the preschool."

"Thanks for calling this in," I told her. "We got

here fast because of it although there's still a lot of damage."

The front of the building was pretty much gone although the back room still stood.

"I didn't call it in," she said, looking around with worry and not at her destroyed school.

I looked to Huck. Emergency dispatch was a county run office down in Helena. The call hadn't come directly to his station.

"She didn't," Huck confirmed. "Kelsey did."

Irene spun in a full circle. "Oh God, where is she?"

"Kelsey?" I asked, even though I knew exactly who Kelsey was. In intimate detail.

"She's with one of my deputies," Huck told her, and she practically wilted in relief.

I looked around although anyone outside of the lights from the emergency vehicles were swallowed by the darkness. I didn't have to search hard because Graham and Kelsey were headed our way. Graham was friends with Thatcher, had played ball with him in high school.

I didn't pay him any attention. I only had eyes for Kelsey, who had her eyes on me as well. I took in her wild hair, her tank top and tiny shorts. She'd clearly been in bed. The way she had her arms crossed over her chest in the middle of all this, she wasn't wearing a bra and trying to hide that fact.

Irene went over to Kelsey and pulled her in for a hug. "God, I was so worried!"

"I'm fine," Kelsey said, reassuring the woman, giving her her full attention. "I got out, no problem."

Got out? My walkie talkie squawked, someone calling for Incident Command, which was me. I had to step away, but I kept my eyes on Kelsey.

When done, I went over to her, took her hand and tugged her away. I gave Huck a glance over my shoulder as we went but didn't give a shit if he wanted to question her.

I had questions for Kelsey, and I wanted answers. Now.

I led her to the back of the fire truck. I sat on the bumper, dropped my jacket beside me, spread my legs and pulled her, so she stood between them. She was cast in shadow, but I could see she was looking at the front of my t-shirt.

Jake, one of the firefighters, came around the side of the truck. "Sorry."

"No worries. Hey, take over IC," I told him.

"Sure thing, Chief."

I didn't look away from Kelsey the entire time. "Okay, sugar. You were the one who called 9-1-1?"

"Yes."

"What did you mean when you said you *got out fine*?"

She sighed. "Because... because I was in the building."

"What are you talking about? Why were you in the preschool in the middle of the night? In... that? Were you sleeping there?" I pointed to her outfit. She said nothing, only pursed her lips together. "Why are you being like this?"

"Like what?"

"Angry," I said, my voice going up. I was angry too. I didn't understand this woman. She ran hot and cold, and I seemed to drive her crazy just by breathing. "Earlier at the community center too. I don't understand what happened. I thought things were good between us. You remember the stable, right?"

She uncrossed her arms and flung them in the air. I'd been right. No bra. Her hard nipples cast dark shadows on her tank top. "Sawyer... I don't know what to say.""

I ran a hand down my face, tired and realizing I was never going to understand women. Not women, one *woman* in particular.

"Something's going on. Please tell me."

Irene came around the truck and stopped, setting

her hand on her chest. Her eyes held a mixture of worry and determination, all of it focused on Kelsey. "You'll stay with me. No arguments."

I looked between the two, saw the way Kelsey's eyes flared wide.

She waited for Kelsey to nod. "Good. I'll be with the police until you're ready." She disappeared into the darkness.

"Why the hell do you need to stay with Irene?"

"Because," she began, then ran a hand over her face. I thought maybe she'd tell me, but she only said, "Just because."

I leaned against the back of the fire truck, exhausted. "Fuck, sugar. Are we even friends?"

Her mouth dropped open. "What?"

"I know what you taste like." I ran my thumb back and forth over the bare skin of her stomach where the tank top had ridden up. Her skin was so fucking soft. Like silk. "I thought maybe we were at least friends. More even. I don't sixty-nine my friends."

"I..." she trailed off, for once at a loss of what to say. I took advantage and pressed on.

"Let me help you."

That seemed to be the wrong fucking thing because she stepped back, shook her head and started to walk off. What the fuck?

I hopped up and chased after her. She'd headed away from the scene and into the darkness.

I grabbed her hand and stopped her. She whirled around, her hair swirling around her bare shoulders.

"I don't want your help!" she hissed.

"Well, you're going to get it," I said, leaning down and tossing her over my shoulder.

She pounded her fists on my lower back. "Sawyer! You can't keep doing this."

I was taking her back to the ranch. Dealing with this shit where she couldn't keep bolting. I started toward the road to my truck and realized I'd driven the fucking fire engine. "Fuck!" I shouted into the night.

"Brother." Huck appeared, one of the emergency vehicle's headlights silhouetting him. "Got a problem?"

"I'm taking Kelsey home with me, but she's not being cooperative."

"I'm right here," she snapped. "Put me down, you Neanderthal."

Huck arched a brow and slowly shook his head as if he was thinking of revoking my man card. I couldn't help but grin in return because he'd find his woman and would be in some kind of fuck-all situation like this. Payback would be a bitch.

"I need to talk with her," he said, using his cop voice.

"Get in line," I countered, not caring about his reason. "But like I said, cooperation isn't her thing."

"I'm still right here!" she shouted, pinching my back above the top of my bunker pants.

Huck looked at Kelsey's upturned ass, and I realized she only had on tiny sleep shorts. His gaze shifted to me, then rolled his eyes. "You owe me one," he said.

I frowned, but he continued. "Kelsey Benoit, you're under arrest for suspicion of arson."

She stiffened on my shoulder.

My eyes widened. "What the fuck, dude?"

"You want to question your woman but can't control her? I'd say she's not going to escape if she's behind bars."

I caught on fast and couldn't help but grin at Huck. Yeah, I owed him one. She was going to tell me what the fuck was going on. All of it. She'd stay in jail until she did.

9

ELSEY

"I REALLY DON'T LIKE YOU," I said to Huck Manning through the bars of the cell. He held out a navy t-shirt, and I snagged it then worked it over my head and arms. It had The Bend Police in big letters on the front and hung down mid-thigh. My feet were still bare, but at least my braless state wasn't quite as obvious now.

"Doesn't matter," he replied. His arms were crossed over his chest, his stance wide. His gaze raked over me, and he nodded, seemingly to himself that I was covered.

Sawyer had carried me over to Huck's police SUV

and ensured I climbed in—to the front passenger seat —and put my seatbelt on. Since the preschool had burned down, I was pretty much out of a job, but being put in the backseat of a police car in front of a group of small town lookiloos, I'd never be able to work with kids again. I was thankful he understood that. Thankfully, Huck had as well and hadn't slapped any cuffs on me.

I hadn't said a word while Sawyer did all that. I'd been so angry and frustrated with him, he might need to pour water over my head about the smoke coming out of my ears. He hadn't said anything, just checked that my belt was secure, gave me a look that I hadn't been able to read, then walked off and got back to work. He was the fire chief, and there'd been a fire.

As for me and Huck, we didn't talk the half a mile to the police station or when he led me to the only jail cell in the place. I wasn't sure if it was because he wasn't a man of many words or because he didn't talk to people he arrested. He hadn't read me my rights like they did on cop shows.

"It's whether you like my brother that matters," he added. A voice came through the walkie talkie on his hip, and he turned it down, not looking away from me. He had the same pale blue eyes as Sawyer.

"I'm not sure if I like him right now either," I

replied, frowning and taking in the bare space. This was definitely a first.

Huck ran a hand back and forth over his head as he studied me.

"I didn't set the fire," I told him.

"I know."

My mouth fell open. "Then why am I here?"

"Because while you may not like him, Sawyer likes *you.*"

"So you arrested me for him?"

"Yup." He turned and walked off, down the short hallway and through the door that led to the main room of the station. This wasn't a big city. The building was old and small and didn't appear to get much use.

There wasn't any noise except for the muffled ringing of a phone and air through a vent in the ceiling. I sat on the bed, careful to sit on the edge and very daintily. I had no idea who or why the last person had been in here.

I hadn't even settled onto the scratchy blanket before I heard the door open, heavy footsteps, and then Sawyer appeared. He was winded, as if he'd run from the fire scene. He'd ditched his thick fire pants and boots and was now in jeans and fire t-shirt. Soot coated his face and neck. I couldn't get over how attractive he was. Earlier, in his gear, he'd been like a calendar model.

I popped up. "Sawyer Manning, get me out of here."

He looked me over, took in the police t-shirt and my bare legs. His jaw ticked. "Not until we talk. I'm tired of you running."

"Fine," I snapped.

He tipped his head back and laughed. "A woman saying 'fine' means everything but *fine*. Why do you keep pushing me away?"

My shoulders slumped, and I looked down at the concrete floor. I refused to think about the germs that were now on my bare feet. "You're being too nice!"

His eyes widened, and he stared at me for a second surprised by my answer. "You want me to be an asshole?"

I gave a slight shake of my head and closed my eyes. "No. It's... I won't be reliant on a man. My ex was all nice like you're being."

"Reliant? I'm offering to help, not own you."

I blinked my eyes open, saw the exasperation on his face. "What's the difference? I take your help now, but what happens later? I can't do it, Sawyer."

He set his hands on his narrow hips, and I remembered the first time I saw him I admired the way he moved them. Then I remembered other ways he moved them so well, which wasn't helping at all. "Do what? You're the one who bought me. Fucked me. Am I just a dick you can ride? I mean, you tossed me aside earlier. You keep pushing me away. *Running away* from what is really fucking good."

Oh shit. His words were well aimed and pierced my heart. Tears filled my eyes, and I blinked them away. There was no way I was crying here. Now. "I told you before that first time, it meant nothing."

He shook his head, took a step closer to the bars. "Then? Maybe. Maybe it had all been attraction. Need. To taste you, fuck you. Get you out of my system. But now? Now you can say what we have means nothing?"

He was so right. Even the other night in the preschool, I'd been lying to myself. Even then, after just meeting him, it had meant something. I had no idea how since we'd only known each other a few hours, but... I'd felt it even then. I wasn't talking about his dick, either.

"We only met yesterday, and you want me in your bed."

"I do, but I'm not asking you to marry me. Hell, like you said, we just met. But there's something here, and I want to play it out. See what happens."

Still... it was scary as hell. "Don't you get it?" I shouted.

My face was probably flushed, and the way I waved my arms in the air, I probably looked a little wild. Frantic.

Through the bars, he grabbed my shoulders, gave me the slightest of shakes. "No, I fucking don't."

I took a breath, and this time when the tears filled my eyes, they slipped down my cheeks. I frantically wiped at them. "If I let you help me, I'll lose myself."

He stilled, stared.

"Says who?" he asked, all the fight gone from his voice. "You? Fuck, sugar. If I don't have you wet and melting all over my dick, you're so fucking prickly, like a damned cactus. You make it so hard to get close, but you're going to let me in. I want to see you, the real you, like earlier in the stable. Fuck, you're gorgeous when you give yourself to me. Let me make you smile as much as I make you come."

My mouth fell open at all that. God, was he a firefighter or a poet? My pussy clenched, and I was eager for those orgasms.

"I can't give you everything," I admitted. "I can't be my mother, and you can't be my ex."

He lifted a hand and cupped my jaw, swiped my tears away with his thumb. "I see you, sugar. That's the problem, isn't it?"

"I need you to be an asshole," she whispered.

"Not happening," he said, looking at me in a way that said he wasn't arguing about it. "We solved this when you kneed me in the balls."

I couldn't help but huff, softening to him.

"Come on, I'll take you home."

My heart flipped. We were right back where we started. "You can't."

He swore under his breath, and his arms fell back to his sides. "Why not?"

"Will you stop asking me questions?"

"No."

"You're so pushy."

"You're so fucking prickly. Why can't I take you home?"

"Because I don't have one!" I snapped my mouth shut as if the words fell out, which they had.

"What—" He didn't say anything else. He blinked, and then awareness flared. He'd guessed earlier but hadn't put it together until now.

It was that light bulb moment that had me crumbling. Crying. I spun on my heel, so he wouldn't look at me, put my hands over my face.

From one second to the next, I was wrapped in strong arms and pressed into his chest, a big hand cupping the back of my head.

"Wait, how..." I got the words out through the tears.

"Huck didn't lock the cell," Sawyer murmured, kissing the top of my head.

His words had my tears stopping for a second, made me realize I *really* didn't like Huck Manning. But when Sawyer whispered, "Sugar," I started crying all over again.

I had no idea how long I cried for. Or why specifically I was actually doing so. At first, I'd been so frustrated with Sawyer, so angry that he'd been pushing me that I'd told him the truth. Or that Huck had arrested me, so I'd be forced to share my secrets.

At some point, Sawyer sat down with me in his lap and just held me. That had made me cry even more because... God, he felt so good. So strong. I wanted to sink into him, so I had, just let it all out. The cheating ex, the shitty roommate, how I'd fallen for both of them. Even my mother. No matter how hard I tried not to be like her, I couldn't prevent it. I couldn't help the feelings I had for Sawyer. How much I wanted to sink into them and be happy.

I finally stopped, wiped my face on his sooty t-shirt. He stroked my hair back and tipped my head, so I met his eyes.

"You called 9-1-1 because you were in the fucking fire because you've been staying in the preschool?"

I nodded.

"For how long?"

"A few weeks."

"Why didn't you say anything?" he asked. All of his earlier frustration was gone.

"I got myself into a mess, and I was going to get myself out."

"Tell me. All of it. And don't even think of bickering about it. We're a little past that now."

I sniffed then rubbed my nose. "I told you I followed a guy here, that he was married."

"Yeah." His jaw clenched, but he didn't say anything else.

"I'd quit my job in Colorado, found someone to sublet my apartment. I had all my stuff in a rental trailer and came up here. I couldn't go back after I learned the truth." I took a deep breath, not thrilled to relive my fuck up. "Online, I found someone who was looking for a roommate, got the job at the preschool. Two months in, I came home from work and discovered she'd moved out. Took her stuff. And mine. Left me with a mattress on the floor, my clothes. I think if we were the same size, she'd have taken those too. And she took my rent money."

"Here in The Bend?"

I shook my head. "No, in Floyd." The town was ten miles away. "I couldn't pay the rent, not my half and certainly not my roommate's half as well. I was evicted, and since I was broke, I had no place to go."

"What about asking your parents for money or savings or—"

I shook my head and wiped away a strand of hair that stuck to my wet cheek. "I never knew my father, and my mom texted earlier asking for rent money. Ironic, huh?"

"That's why you were so upset at the community center earlier?"

I nodded. "I got her message after we left the ranch. The Phoenix guy dumped her."

"What about savings?" he asked.

"Student loans have sapped me, but what little I had saved went to the move, so there wasn't enough for a deposit on a new place." I dropped my forehead against his chest. "I was an idiot."

He ran a hand over my hair. "You trusted. That's not being an idiot. What did you do?"

"I already had the job here at the preschool, so I was getting a paycheck but not fast enough to get a place to live. A motel was too expensive for more than a night. Irene figured out what happened. She let me stay at her place. I slept on the couch. One of her kids put peanut butter on my nose while I was sleeping. I smeared it on my face, and I woke up to one of her dogs licking it off. Obviously, her house is insane. I asked if I could crash in the preschool until I got back on my feet. I figure another few weeks, and I'd be able to get a place on my own. Now though..."

"You're coming home with me."

I wanted to say yes. So bad. Instead, I shook my head. "I can't," I whispered.

He tugged on my hair, so I looked at him again. It wasn't painful, but the pull reminded me of how in control he could be, especially when we were naked. "Can't or won't?"

"I have no place to live. I obviously have no job now. I can't just go home with you and have you take care of me. It's the one thing I've tried to avoid."

"Having someone take care of you?" He looked... bewildered, as if I were speaking another language. "It's okay to rely on people."

"Like I relied on my ex and ended up stuck in Montana? Like my mother moves in with a guy, gets dumped and is homeless without any money?"

"Stop comparing me to your ex. You can stay with me until you get your apartment. No strings."

I shook my head and pushed off his lap. He let me

go but tangled his fingers with mine as if wanting to keep touching me. I wanted to run, especially with the cell's door open. It was exactly what I wanted to do although the pull to climb right back in his lap was just as strong.

I didn't want to walk out into the main part of the police station and face Huck either. The ass.

Sawyer didn't understand. He had two brothers. A housekeeper who seemed to care about all three of them enough to auction them off in the hope of finding love. He was Seesaw. He'd never be alone.

I looked to him, the seriousness in his eyes, the way he looked at *me,* as if I mattered. As if I was *his.* He belonged on the cover of a firefighter calendar. And that five o'clock shadow that was *way* past five o'clock. He was that handsome. He didn't even know it. Or care. "No, because when you're done with me, I'll be worse off than I am now. My mom—"

"You're not your mom. Whatever fucked up shit your mom's done to your head, you aren't reliant on me. Beholden."

"You're rich. I don't want your money, Sawyer. I wish you didn't have it because then I wouldn't have to worry that if things fall apart, I won't be able to stand on my own two feet."

"When I'm done with you? When things fall apart?

I don't like that you're planning the end of our relationship."

"Relationship? I've known you less than two days."

"Yes, *relationship*," he repeated. "This is it for me. *You're* it for me. If it takes telling you every day for a long, long time to prove it, I will. Maybe I can fuck you into believing me because the only time you're not fighting me is when my dick's in you."

I sniffed then smiled because it was actually true. "I... I think you're right."

The corner of his mouth turned up, and I felt his muscles relax. "About which part?"

He lowered his head, so he was blurry, but his lips hovered right above mine.

"Definitely about your dick being in me, but maybe... all of it?"

After I admitted that, he kissed me. Not gently. Fierce, as if he had to get all his feelings out all at once. His hands went to my hips to turn me, so I straddled his waist. He broke the kiss long enough to tug the t-shirt over my head. "You wear a guy's shirt, you wear mine. No police t-shirts for my woman," he said, staring at my nipples which were hard and *very* visible through my tank top.

Huck cleared his throat, and I startled, whipping my head toward him standing outside the cell. I pulled the crumpled t-shirt in front of my chest although he and half the town had had more than an eyeful at the fire.

"You two can have make up sex later and preferably not in my jail cell. The fire damage was mostly to the front of the building. Graham and Irene got your things and brought your car over."

I hadn't even thought of that, which meant Irene must have told him I'd been staying there. "Thank you."

Huck gave a small nod then looked to Sawyer. "It's my turn to talk with her."

"Now?" Sawyer asked, his fingers tightening on my hips in what felt like a possessive gesture.

"You were there when the guy started the fire." His face was serious as he set his hands on his hips as his pale gaze was focused squarely on me. He had the same intensity as Sawyer, the same *HeMan* save-the-world vibe.

"Yes."

"Did you see the guy start it?"

"Yes," I repeated. "He tossed something through the front window. It woke me up. The main room was on fire. I peeked out the front, saw him with a can and pouring the contents on the building. Gas, I guess. He tossed a match, and it caught right away, then he took off. Drove away."

"Fuck," Sawyer breathed, and he ran a hand down my spine.

"I went out the back then called 9-1-1."

Sawyer sucked in a breath, took hold of my chin, so I had to look him in the eye. "You saw him clearly?"

Gone was the sweet and sexy guy. In his place was the protective, bossy replacement.

I shrugged. "I saw him, but never saw his face. Dark pants, hoodie. I can't identify him."

"What about the car?" Huck asked.

I replied right away with what I remembered. "White or silver. Older model. Four door. The back quarter panel was a different color as if it had been replaced."

"She's staying with me," Sawyer said. He lifted me off his lap then stood. "This is a small town. Word's going to spread this was arson. Everyone will know before their first cup of coffee."

This time, when he tugged me down the hall, I didn't protest.

10

AWYER

AFTER OUR LITTLE come-to-Jesus chat, I'd followed her back to the ranch. She hadn't argued, maybe because it was after two in the morning by the time we'd showered off the fire and settled in my bed. I hadn't done more than pull her into my arms before she fell asleep. I'd kissed her head and reveled in the feel of her in my house, in my bed before I passed out too.

Huck had woken us early. Too fucking early. Told us to come to the station. That they'd found the guy who'd set the fire. I'd wanted to spend the morning with Kelsey. In my bed. Naked. But I wanted this fire mess behind us. I wanted to ensure Kelsey wasn't in any danger.

She'd grabbed clean clothes from the trunk of her car, and I'd driven us into town.

As she wrote out her statement about the fire, I grabbed coffees at the cafe down the block. What she'd shared the night before still stuck with me. She had serious hang-ups about relationships and men. I'd told her she was mine, and I'd get her to come around. Words didn't seem to work with her. Action would. Patience, too. It had truly been two days. I needed to let things just happen. Enjoy the ride. But a fucking fire made for a bumpy road. And the fact that she'd been living in the preschool with only Irene in the know.

"Can you think of anything else at all?" Huck asked as I came in, setting her paper on top of a small pile he had going.

I set the cardboard carrier on Huck's desk and passed the cups around. Dropped into the empty seat.

Kelsey shook her head. While she looked beautiful to me, she looked exhausted. A few hours of sleep wasn't enough since she had dark circles under her eyes.

She'd been in a fire. Fuck me, that made my blood chill because I'd seen what happened to people who didn't get out in time. It made me want to pull her onto my lap and never let her up.

She took a tentative sip of her coffee.

Huck leaned back in his chair, sighed. I had no idea if he'd even gone back to the ranch for a few hours of shuteye. He interlaced his fingers behind his neck, elbows sticking out. "You haven't seen anyone around the preschool during the past week? Checking it out?"

We sat in the two utilitarian chairs across from him. His office was vintage eighties, the fake leather the color of pumpkins. The carpet matched although worn.

"No. We're careful about that because of the kids."

"Off hours?" he asked, dropping his arms and leaning forward. He took the lid off his to-go cup and tossed it in the trash. He meant when she'd been staying there.

She shrugged. "No although I haven't paid attention."

Huck wiped his hand down his face.

"You said you found the guy," I said, eyeing my brother.

He nodded. "We had a call around four. Rollover

out on the county road. White four-door sedan. Back quarter panel had been replaced, just like you said."

The fire department would have been called out, but I hadn't been on duty. I was sure there was a report at the station, and I could get a rundown from those who responded.

Kelsey sat upright. "Is the driver okay?"

A nerve ticked in Huck's jaw. "He was ejected. No seatbelt. DOA. Alcohol was involved. Besides stinking of liquor, the dead guy reeked of gasoline. Plus there was a gas can inside."

"You think it was the arsonist?" I asked although the answer was pretty obvious.

Huck glanced my way. "Based on Kelsey's eyewitness account of the car, the fact that there was a gas can... it's looking that way."

"ID?"

"Alan Dunsmore. Idaho driver's license." He looked to Kelsey. "Name ring a bell?"

She shook her head.

"We'll be looking into him, and the case stays open."

A quick knock, and Graham stuck his head in the door. "Chief. Bunky's here."

Huck nodded, then the deputy disappeared.

"What the hell is Bunky doing here?" I asked.

Huck stood, adjusted his utility belt. Sighed loudly. Glanced longingly at his ditched coffee. "He owns the preschool building. Needs the police report to file an insurance claim."

"Think he knows the guy? Enemy?" I asked.

Huck shrugged, letting his shoulders droop in obvious weariness over having to deal with the guy. I didn't blame him. "It's possible, but this doesn't seem like Bunky. If he wanted the insurance money, blatant arson's not the way to go. I doubt they'll pay out. Now he's got a fire damaged building not bringing in any rent. Plus, he's got to rebuild. That shit's expensive and all out of his pocket."

Going around the desk, Huck left us in his office.

"Bunky?" Kelsey asked, setting her drink beside Huck's.

"A guy we grew up with," I said, taking a big swig of my drink. I liked my coffee black and this time I got a double shot added. Even that wasn't going to fortify me if I had to deal with Tom Bunker. "He was in my class at school but was held back in sixth grade, so he ended up being between me and Huck. I don't have all that much good to say about the guy. His parents owned a bunch of properties in town. When they died, he inherited it all. I didn't know the preschool was one of his places though." I sighed, glad Huck had to deal with him and not me. "I'm hungry. Want to grab some lunch?"

"Sure."

We left Huck's office and headed toward the entrance. Kelsey stopped short, and I almost bumped into her, setting a hand on her shoulder.

"Sugar?"

Over her shoulder, I could see her staring wide-eyed at Bunky and Huck, who were talking in the lobby's small waiting area. Bunky looked like he'd just stepped off a golf course in his pressed khakis and pale blue golf shirt. His dark hair was receding, and he kept it long on the top to hide that fact. He was a decent looking guy, but in a rich asshole sort of way.

Color drained from her face, and I gave her a squeeze. She blinked, but didn't offer any other response.

Oh shit.

"What's the matter? He's not the guy you saw, is it?" Maybe my question to Huck had been dead right. It made sense. A sloppy arson. A guy burning down his own place. I had no idea why Bunky would be hurting for cash. Besides the land he'd inherited, his mother had been some kind of oil heiress, and the money trickled down to him in some kind of trust. He wouldn't know hard work if it hit him in the face.

Thus, his repeat of sixth grade. But if he wanted the insurance money, Huck was right. Insurance didn't cover crimes like that, and now he was stuck with a useless piece of land.

She shook her head, which meant Bunky wasn't an arsonist as well as an asshole.

It took only another two seconds for Huck to look our way, which distracted Bunky, and he turned as well. He stopped talking mid-sentence. His dark eyes widened, which meant he was just as surprised to see Kelsey as she was on him.

"Kelsey?" Bunky asked. "It's... good to see you."

The words came out faker than his tan.

"Yeah, *Bunky.*"

By Kelsey's tone, she didn't like the guy. She had good taste.

He gave a smile. "Old nickname. I go way back with the Mannings."

"Tom Bunker," Kelsey said, as if it finally made sense. Whatever it was.

"You two know each other?" Huck asked, looking between the two as if in a tennis match.

"We know each other," Bunky said, setting his hand on his hips. "She tried to break up my marriage last year."

What. The. Fuck?

Kelsey stiffened then took a deep breath, tipped her chin up. "You mean when you wanted to spend the rest of our lives together? When you said I should move here to be with you?"

Bunky was Kelsey's Tom? The ex who'd turned out to be married? Tom Bunker?

Bunky shook his head as if silently scolding a child. "You showed up at my house."

"You said you loved me!" Kelsey was practically vibrating with anger beneath my palms.

Thankfully, the only other person in the lobby to witness this was Graham, and he was at his desk, watching all of it but remaining silent.

Bunky's gaze shifted to my hand on Kelsey's shoulder. Narrowed. Then a grin that could only be classified as twisted spread across his face. "Oh, it's like that?"

"Like what?" I asked, not in the mood for him or his shit.

"Let me give you a piece of advice," he began then tipped his chin up to indicate Kelsey. "This one's a clinger. A gold digger." He laughed then pointed at me. "Oh shit, this is a riot. You sure know how to pick 'em. First Tina, now Kelsey. Women who want you for your money. That's what this one did with me. I'd watch your wallet with this one."

"*This one?*" Kelsey all but shouted.

When she moved toward him, I didn't stop her. My mind had shorted out or something. Bunky's words about Tina hit a raw wound that obviously hadn't healed. The anger that lingered from her using me was like a bitter taste in my mouth. I didn't have feelings for Tina other than extreme dislike. But Bunky used her like a weapon to fuck with me.

Except Kelsey wasn't like Tina. Nothing like her. I knew it. Sure, this was happening fast, whatever *this* was between us. My feelings for Kelsey had gotten serious quick. The same way I'd been with Tina. But if Kelsey had wanted my money, she'd have hopped in my bed instead of doing everything possible to avoid it.

I wasn't angry because I believed Bunky. I didn't believe a thing out of his mouth. I was angry because of the way he smirked when Huck had to grab Kelsey to keep her off him, like he was the civilized one and her rash behavior only validated his comments. I had no doubt she'd have kneed Bunky in the balls for what he'd said if Huck wasn't pinning her to his side.

"Bunky's why you keep pushing me away?" I asked her.

Huck turned and because Kelsey was caught in his hold, she moved with him.

"What?" she whispered. Her cheeks were flushed, and her green eyes wild. She looked to Bunky and narrowed her eyes, then at me.

"Tom Bunker's your ex. The one you compared me to," I said, putting it all together.

Bunky laughed, and I glared. The look didn't stop him like it might have in high school.

"No, I—" she sputtered.

"I can't rely on a guy, you said. I can't tell when one's telling the truth. Those were your words, right?" I spit it out as if my comments tasted bad. "It makes so much more sense now."

"What does?"

I rubbed the back of my neck, feeling the fool. "No wonder you're all fucked up about men. Bunky's a world class user. A rich one."

"Hey!" he said, but I ignored him like always. I glared at Kelsey who wasn't denying it.

I'd hated him since he was a kid. Still did. But to be lumped in with him? Fuck no. I couldn't think of anything worse. I'd tried all my life to be a good guy, a decent guy. To help people. Bunky wouldn't give a life jacket to a child if he needed it to save himself instead.

She blinked.

Her lack of response was more telling than anything she could say.

I took off my Stetson, slapped it against my thigh. Sighed. "You were right. We shouldn't do this. I can't be with a woman who doesn't want *me*. Tina wanted my money."

She fought against Huck's hold, but he wouldn't let her go. "I don't want your money," she cried.

"Oh, I know. You turned down any offer of help. If it were that, it would be so much simpler. But I'm supposedly just like Bunky. Tom fucking Bunker." I pointed at the loser.

"Hey!" he shouted again.

"If you think I'm just like that asshole, even after what we've done together, then I was wrong about you."

"Sawyer," she said, tears filling her eyes.

I held up my hand. "Save it. If you can't tell the difference between a guy who wants what's best for you and a guy who will fuck around on his wife and family and lie, then... I'm done. Good thing, too, before I gave a shit."

The last thing I saw was her mouth fall open. A tear slipped down her cheek.

Bunky laughed.

I stalked over to him, punched him in the nose.

"What the—" he bellowed, his hand going to his

face. He followed that by a string of obscenities. Blood dripped down between his fingers.

"That's for what you did to Kelsey," I snarled. "You so much as talk shit about her to anyone, I'll bury you in the back forty where no one will ever find your sorry ass."

His eyes flared wide then whipped to Huck. "Did you hear that? He threatened me. You're the police chief. Arrest him!"

My knuckles hurt, my heart was pounding, and I was pissed.

"I didn't hear a thing," Huck said, slowly shaking his head.

"He broke my nose!"

Huck shrugged, not giving a shit. "Gotta watch out for the doors in this place. It needs some updates around here. I'll be sure to let the city council know what happened. Maybe we'll get some funds allocated for a remodel."

Bunky's narrow gaze shifted to Graham. "You were a witness."

Graham held up his hands. "Didn't see a thing. You might want to get that looked at."

"Careful with the blood on the carpet," Huck warned. "That's a bitch to get out."

I didn't linger to listen to any more of Bunky's

whining. I gave Kelsey one last look then left. I wasn't sure if it was the sadness on her face or the fact that I'd thought we'd had something that made me feel like total shit. It didn't matter. I'd known Kelsey two days. I'd be able to forget about her just as fast.

Right?

11

 ELSEY

"I'M NOT sure why I'm here," I said, stirring my tomato soup Alice had put in front of me. It looked home-made with bits of herbs and probably cream. I should be more eager for it since I'd survived lately mostly on cheap microwave entrees, but I only felt sad and hurt. I wanted to leave, and my car was parked in front of Sawyer's house, but I had a feeling she'd drag me back by my ear or something.

She set a plate of grilled cheese beside the soup. Dammit. She knew I wasn't going to walk away from butter and melted cheese.

After Sawyer had stormed out of the police station, Huck had handed off Tom—now obviously known to locals as Bunky—to Graham to whine to and file his police report about the fire. Huck had tucked me into his SUV—again—and this time driven me to the ranch. He hadn't said a word the entire way.

He pulled up in front of the big house, not to Sawyer's place. He'd literally walked me to the front door, handed me off to Alice then left.

I had no idea who'd won him at the auction, but I had to hope he wasn't as much of an asshole with her as Sawyer was with me.

Then again, he was protecting his brother, and I appreciated that loyalty. Although why he hadn't just put me back in jail—and locking the cell door this time—or pushed me out onto the station's front steps, I wasn't sure.

"Because you must be hungry," Alice said although it made no sense for him to bring me all the way out here since there were several places to eat in town.

I took a bite of the grilled cheese. Dammit, I couldn't even argue because I was hungry, and the sandwich was incredible. I peered at it, thinking she even buttered and toasted the inner sides of the bread before she put the cheese on.

"I don't think Huck likes me."

She laughed. I guessed Alice was in her sixties, her long hair pulled back in a loose bun at her nape, a rich brown turning toward gray. She was simply dressed in jeans and a burgundy top, but she added flare with a paisley scarf tied loosely over her shoulders. This was the woman who put all three Manning men up for auction, which showed they respected her and also feared her. This was why I didn't leave. If grown men were scared of the woman, I was smart enough not to cross her. She might be small, but I had a feeling she ran this ranch and let the men believe they did.

"I think you're worried about the wrong Manning," she said, using a dish towel to wipe down the already clean counter.

It was clear this part of the house was old from the ceiling beams and well-worn plank flooring, but the kitchen had been updated recently. Claire's artwork was stuck to the fridge. A wall had been taken out and a great room added, allowing for a family room/kitchen combination. Pictures hung on the walls. There was a row of hooks by the back door. Boots stood in a line beside it. This place was lived in. Loved. It was a home. I could imagine Sawyer growing up here, having his parents eat dinner with him and his brothers. His grandparents living in this place before him. And another generation before them.

I sighed, dipped my sandwich half in the soup and took a bite.

She poured herself a cup of coffee then stood on the other side of the center island.

"I don't think Sawyer likes me all that much either."

I swallowed hard, suddenly not all that interested in the meal. I'd hurt Sawyer, and I'd done it intentionally but only because I'd been afraid and tried to push him away.

"He's a big man. Strong. Beneath all that, he's got a tender heart. Probably more so than his brothers."

I'd picked up on that.

"Irene told me what's been going on with you."

I whipped my head up and met her even gaze. I didn't see sympathy in her eyes, the words only stated as fact.

"You didn't have to stay in the preschool. There were many people who would have helped you. Irene included."

I rolled my eyes. "Her son put peanut butter on my face while I was sleeping."

She laughed, put her fingers over her lips. "She told me about that too."

"I need to stand on my own two feet."

Her smile slipped, and she nodded. "I understand

that, and that shows the kind of person you are. But being independent's possible to do while people have your back. Standing on your own two feet is one thing, but you don't have to do it alone."

I frowned, scooped up some soup and ate it, so I didn't have to answer.

"You think Sawyer can't take care of himself just because he's got his brothers to be there for him?" she asked me.

I frowned, thought of Sawyer loaded with responsibility as the fire chief and also on the ranch. To his family. He was strong. Protective. Bossy. "Well... no."

She looked around as if to confirm we were alone. "I'll have you know those three men wouldn't be able to find dinner if it wasn't put before them. They can cook, but they're men."

She paused there, as if that answered everything.

"They rely on me, probably more than they ever realize," she added. "It doesn't make them less, it makes them family. We take care of each other."

"I have my mother, but she's not what you'd call... *maternal.* The last time she texted, she asked for rent money, which I find ironic." I shoved a big bite of sandwich in my mouth.

"Blood doesn't always make a family, Kelsey," she said then took a sip of her coffee. "Sawyer's a helper."

When I finally finished chewing and swallowing, I said, "He wants to *save* me. I really, really need to save myself."

"You saved him from Delilah."

I shrugged. "That's different."

"Sawyer, Huck and Thatcher are all a little afraid of Delilah. Let me tell you a story about that one." She pursed her lips as if she was sucking on a lemon. Then she proceeded to tell me about how she'd climbed in Sawyer's bedroom window when he was in high school. "She didn't succeed then or now."

I could picture Delilah as a teenager being so bold. I could also see now why Sawyer had been extra thankful I'd won him in the auction.

"You need to know some things about Sawyer. About Huck, too. Thatcher as well, but he doesn't show it as much."

I stirred the corner of my sandwich around in my soup and took another bite. "Okay."

"You heard their momma and daddy died."

I nodded.

Sadness flitted across her lined face. "The boys were young when it happened. Sawyer was fifteen. The others even younger. One day Paul and Carolyn were just... gone. Sawyer, Huck and Thatcher were crazy boys." She laughed then sighed. "What boys aren't crazy? They did things like what Irene's son did to you."

I could only imagine what kind of hellions those three were like.

"But after the crash, they got serious. Maybe too serious. Learned quick what was important. I'd say Sawyer and Huck went into the careers they did because of their parents' deaths. They couldn't save them, so they're going to try their darndest to save everyone else."

"Oh," I breathed. That made sense. Too much so.

"I think that's why he fell so hard for his ex, Tina. Had stars in his eyes and missed that she was a schemer." Her mouth turned down into a frown. "She wasn't for him."

"So Sawyer wasn't trying to help me specifically, it's just the way he is."

She laughed, waved her hand. "Honey, he helps the ones he cares about the most."

I let that sink in. Had he tried to help me because he cared about me? That's what normal people did. But I'd pushed it away because I wasn't normal. I was feeling more like an idiot by the minute.

And it only got worse. "Sawyer's not mad about all that though," I admitted.

"Oh?"

"I... I compared him to Tom Bunker."

She stared at me wide eyed. I had a feeling I'd surprised the woman, and it wasn't something easily done. Not after raising the three Mannings. "Bunky?"

I nodded. I never knew Tom by that name, but it made sense, and it made him sound like a country bumpkin. Which he was, even in his golf shirts.

"Why?"

"Because he was the guy who lied about being in love with me, why I followed him to Montana."

"Oh, honey."

I ran a hand over my face, suddenly weary. I was exhausted.

"That makes more sense. Why Sawyer's mad, I mean. The only thing he and Bunky have in common is that they have penises."

I'd just taken a bite of sandwich, and I coughed. Sadly, I could confirm her statement, but there was no comparison.

"That boy is... well, he's an asshole."

I'd never expected her to swear, but there wasn't any other word for it. "I agree."

"If you think he's an asshole, why did you compare them?"

I told her about how I'd fallen for Tom, followed him, learned the truth about him.

She frowned more and more as I went on and grabbed an apple and a knife from the drawer and started slicing it up.

"Sawyer's nothing like Bunky." The words came out in a tone that made my comparison almost an insult of her child rearing abilities.

"I know, but... I kept pushing him away." I pushed my hair back behind my ear. "After Tom... Bunky, I don't trust men."

"I don't blame you. What he did was wrong. His wife has to know what he's up to. She has to be lingering for the money."

"Yeah. My mother always found the worst apple in the bunch." I said the last because she placed some slices on my plate. "I think it's hereditary."

"People make bad choices all the time. It's whether you learn from them that's important," she told me pointing the knife at me.

"My mom sure hasn't."

"Then it's not hereditary because you have."

"I have horrible luck. The preschool burned down. God, maybe I'm cursed."

"I think you're a little hard on yourself. And Sawyer," she added.

"I had no place to live, and Sawyer would have offered if he knew the truth, which would have made me just like her. What would have happened once he dumped me?"

"Why would he do that?" She looked almost bewildered I even suggested the possibility.

"I've known him two days!"

"So?"

I tipped my chin down and gave her a level stare. "I bought him at an auction."

"Exactly."

"Exactly," I repeated, now completely confused. I eyed her, unsure. "Are you agreeing with me?"

"Did Sawyer say he wants to keep you?"

"Not in those exact words but yes." I flushed, remembering. *I'm your man. This pussy's mine. You're it for me.* Definitely words I wasn't going to share.

"Then he will. But that doesn't mean he's taking over your life. He wants to join his with yours."

Still... "I can't move in with him."

"Then don't."

"I don't have a place to live. Heck, with the preschool burned down, I don't even have a job."

"The preschool's going to be run from one of the rooms at the community center. Until the building's redone or Irene chooses another location. You're not the only one who needs the preschool to stay open. Who's accepted help," she added, giving me a pointed look. Irene must have been offered the space and taken it, taken the help that had been freely given.

People moved fast around here.

"Wow, okay. That's... good to hear."

"As for a place to live, there are enough beds on this ranch to sleep in instead of his, if that's what you want. Do you think I'm going to let you stay anywhere else until you get back on your feet? Think Thatcher or Huck would either?" She went back to the coffee maker and topped off her cup.

"Huck might."

She glanced over her shoulder at me. "Huck brought you here. I think he wants you with Sawyer more than you think."

I wasn't so sure about that.

"Honey, do you want Sawyer?" she asked, coming back to the spot she had and leaned forward, resting her forearms on the counter.

I licked my lips, thought about it. Then stopped thinking about it. There wasn't much to consider. My heart knew the truth better than my head. Maybe that was what had gotten me so screwed up in the first place.

He'd punched Tom... Bunky in the face defending my honor *after* he'd broken up with me.

"Yes. But he said he didn't give a sh—sugar about me." I blushed at my cussing.

A smile spread across her face. "I think I've heard that word before. I won't faint dead away. If he didn't give a sugar, then why was he so upset?"

I blinked, thought about it. If Sawyer didn't care about me, about whatever it was between us, then he would have shrugged it off. He didn't. Far from it. Was Alice right? Did he care so much that I'd truly hurt him?

"Get some rest, honey. I'll show you to Huck's room, so you can take a nap. The boy's not going anywhere. Let him work off his mad for a little while."

"He's really upset," I told her.

She came around the counter, patted me on the arm. "I'm sure you can think of a way to fix that."

An idea did come to me based on what she'd told me about Delilah. Could it work? Would Sawyer be receptive or toss me out?

12

*S*AWYER

I WALKED from Thatcher's place in the old barn back to my place, the moon lighting my way. When I left Kelsey at the station, I'd driven back to the ranch. Pissed. I'd come across my brother, and he'd dragged me out on four-wheelers to ride the fence line. We spent the rest of the day fixing shit. Digging holes, hammering nails, running barbed wire.

Thatcher might be considered the *easygoing* one of the three Manning brothers, but he knew when to keep his mouth shut. When he'd first asked after Kelsey with his signature grin, I'd glared and asked him after the woman who'd bought him at the auction. That had wiped the look off his face and shut him right up. I had no idea what the story was there, but I wasn't going to push because I didn't want him to push right back. So we'd spent the day talking only about the land. I'd gone back to his place for dinner and a beer, watching a stupid car chase movie to pass the time.

I didn't want to be in my house where Kelsey had been. I had no doubt her sweet scent would be lingering, ready to drive me fucking insane. I was already out of sorts. Angry. Restless.

As I climbed the porch steps to the kitchen door, I tried to figure out how a woman I'd known for two days could bend me so far out of shape. No, that was wrong. I knew exactly how Kelsey had done it. I'd fallen for her, first glance.

That smile. That red fucking hair. Her sass. Even the way she'd kneed my balls. Then, once I got her bare, I couldn't get enough. I loved her body. Her curves. The way she responded to me. We had serious chemistry, but more importantly, a connection. Something... lasting.

I just knew. I wanted her. I still did, even with her hang-ups and issues.

I unlocked the door, pushed inside, tugged my

boots off and left them beside the door. Set my hat on the hook.

I shouldn't be bent out of shape that she'd been with Bunky. I hadn't known her then. She was just one of many who'd fallen for his shit. I wanted to break his nose all over again for how he treated her. Out of all the things I could do in this moment, that was one of them. My fists clenched, wishing he was around.

I cut through the dark house to my bedroom. There it was, in the air. Her scent.

"Fuck," I whispered then paused and took a deep breath.

As for Bunky, I should actually be thanking the little shit. If not for him, I'd never have met Kelsey. There was no fucking way I would admit that aloud to anyone, especially since I couldn't get her to see that I was nothing like that fucker. She'd have to do it on her own. I'd given her enough examples of what kind of man I was. How I'd treat her. How we'd be together.

She had to come to me.

I just didn't know if she would.

At the bedroom doorway, I flicked on the light.

Froze.

There she was, sprawled across my bed. Naked. Eating directly from a carton of ice cream. She pulled the spoon from her mouth, licked it with her tongue.

"Holy shit," I murmured.

My heart skipped a beat. My dick went instantly hard. I couldn't move. The sight of her... fuck me. Her clothes were a pile on the floor beside the bed. She was laying on her side, the sheet seductively pulled over her but didn't cover any of the important spots, like that fiery thatch of curls that covered her pinkest of places. I watched her nipples harden. I knew those curves. I'd kissed and licked and—

Her smile slipped a little when I continued to just stare.

"I hope you don't mind, your window was open."

I looked to the open window, imagined her climbing through.

"I figure if Delilah could do it, I could manage. Maybe I'll be a little more successful than she was."

I reached down, adjusted myself. "My dick's hard. I'd say that's a good start."

I'd always pictured my woman in my bed but never knew who it was. For a little while, I'd thought it had been Tina, but what I felt for that psycho in six months of dating could fill a thimble in comparison to what I felt for Kelsey in two days.

I knew now. No question. I wasn't going to tell Kelsey that though. Not yet. I might have zero doubts that she was the one, but she hadn't come to the same conclusion yet. She was right. We'd only known each other *two* days. Two fucking days, and my world had changed.

I was keeping her. I had the rest of our lives to convince her.

Last night, we'd been too exhausted to do more than climb beneath the covers and conk out.

Now? Now it was time to make things right then make her mine.

She set the spoon in the carton, placed that on the bedside table. Then, with so much fucking shame, she sat up and held the sheet over her body.

"I'm sorry," she said, her green eyes on mine. "I know you're nothing like Tom... Bunky. But you're a guy, and I've been wary of all guys. And you came on so strong. So fucking nice, and it scared me."

The words were coming out in a tumble.

"And sneaking into my house, into my bed isn't coming on strong?" I countered.

Those slim shoulders went up and down. "I'd hoped—" She stopped, glanced away then started again. "It makes no sense that I'm afraid of how you make me feel when everything is good while I ditched my life in another state to follow an asshole."

"How do I make you feel?" I asked, cutting to the most important part of what she said.

She finally looked at me, her head tipped back. I saw the torment, the worry in her eyes. "It's happening really fast."

"And yet you're in my bed."

She glanced down at it, a little frown forming in her brow as if she were second guessing her bold presence.

"I.... I—"

"It's not happening, sugar. It's done. One look, and I knew." Okay, so I wasn't going to play it cool after all. She was... In. My. Bed. *In my fucking bed.* Naked. I went over to her, sat down on the mattress, shifted to face her. "There's nothing to be afraid of in that. You should be reassured."

She pulled her mouth to the side as if considering. Hard.

"I'm not going to drop you," I added. "Ever. I'll always catch you."

She shook her head slowly. "You're a romantic."

I laughed then. "Again, you're in my bed. Who's the romantic one?"

She rolled her eyes, and her mouth turned up in a smile.

"You think Alice would let me be a dick to you?" I continued. "Think Huck would lock me up? Thatcher'd take me out into the south forty and shoot me." I paused, wondering why he hadn't earlier while we were out there for leaving her at the station.

She didn't say anything, but I saw that my self-deprecation made her eyes sparkle.

"As for being a romantic? I think only with you. How about this? I want your body." I let my gaze drop and rake over her, so mussed and perfect beneath my sheet. "I want to be *in* your body. If I could be inside you all day long, I would." I reached out, picked up the spoon from the ice cream carton then dropped it. "I want all the ice cream cones with you."

She blushed and huffed out a laugh.

"I'm not joking."

She flung herself at me. Fortunately, my balls were safe. She wrapped her arms around my neck and kissed the hell out of me. An oomph escaped, and she used my surprise for her tongue to find mine.

My arms wrapped around her as the sheet fell to her waist. Her body was warm and lush beneath my palms.

In an instant, I took over the kiss.

Fuck, yes. She tasted of vanilla cream and every dark desire.

Kelsey'd been willing before, but now... now she was right there with me. *In. My. Bed.*

This was our first kiss. The real one where we were

both in this thing together. It meant something. It *was* something.

She lifted her head, blinked, then her eyes met mine filled with warmth and need. "I want all the ice cream cones with you, too."

I stroked her hair back. "Good."

"I'm not fixed, Sawyer." Her soft breath fanned my cheek. "Being with you isn't going to make my feelings change."

"Not right away. Over time," I countered. "Bunky's an asshole."

"With a broken nose," she said.

I smirked because I was very pleased with that, and her eyes held something that looked like glee.

"You'll learn being with me, as part of the Manning family, how much of a shit head he is. Then you'll thank him."

She leaned back as if she'd thought I said we were moving to the moon. "*Thank* him?"

I nodded and absently ran a finger over the line of her collarbone then lower to circle a nipple. It hardened before my eyes. "Yeah, we'll add him to our holiday card list because he brought us together."

Her lips pursed, and she gave me a skeptical look. "My mother's going to be a long-term problem."

I pulled my hand away, not wanting to talk about anyone's mother while I played with her nipple.

"She's not going away. You can't punch her in the nose."

"When she texts again—"

"Which she will," she added.

"Then you'll show it to me. We'll talk it out. Not let it affect us."

"That simple?"

I huffed out a laugh. "Family's not simple, that's for fucking sure. But like you protected me from Delilah, I'll protect you, too."

"When you put it that way..."

"It's settled."

She laughed. "Just like that?"

I shrugged, content. Fucking happy. "You're in my bed where you belong."

She squirmed, her tits shifting, and my dick ached to get in her. To have no clothes separating us. We were halfway there.

"This isn't happily ever after," she said. "Even if you do have puppies."

I wasn't going to contradict her. I would prove her wrong in about fifty years. My parents' marriage had been solid. Sure, they had problems. Three boys who must've made them nuts. But I remembered them laughing. Kissing in the kitchen. My dad pulling my momma into a corner for a little more than a smooch. They'd had their happily ever after, even if it had been cut short.

"Fine, then, happy for now," I said instead. I'd take it one day at a time, and the two so far with this woman... well, it had been a fucking roller coaster, but it seemed I liked that kind of ride.

She took some time to contemplate my words. "Happy for now is good. But I... I want my own place," she blurted as her eyes met mine.

I cocked my head. This was important to her. Even though I wanted to keep her right where she was, *just* as she was, it couldn't happen. "Okay. You can be mine and still have your own apartment."

"Really?" she asked, clearly surprised.

Yeah, we had work to do. "I get it. Your own space. Standing on your own two feet, especially after what happened."

"Exactly. Alice says I'm staying in the big house until then."

"Let me guess, she put you in Huck's old room."

She frowned. "Yes, why?"

"Because it's on the ground floor, and she wanted you to sneak out and come here."

"She did not," she countered, as if she couldn't imagine Alice matchmaking.

"She told you about Delilah and what she did in high school."

"Yeah."

I tipped my head and gave her a look that screamed, *See?*

Her hand smacked my chest. She thought I was joking. "I mean it. You having your own bed doesn't mean I won't be sleeping in it. Or you tonight in mine."

She tipped her head, squinted up at me. "I guess that's true."

"Being with me doesn't make you anything like your momma, sugar," I told her, reiterating this because like she said, her issues with the woman weren't going to end just because she was in my arms... or bed. "I heard the preschool's going to relocate to the community center for a while, so you have a job. Soon you'll have your own place. Like you had in Colorado before Bunky, right?"

She sighed. "Yes. I wasn't this crazy then."

"You sure?" I asked, tipping her chin up.

"You think I'm crazy?" I had been the night before, but now, when I had all the answers? No.

"You're in my bed. Just like Delilah was back in high school."

"I bought you to *save* you from Delilah," she countered. "I just... need to be sure. If I don't take a little time to be good at being me, then I'll never know."

That made sense, and I respected her for it.

She glanced away. "The fire scared me though. I'm actually really glad to be staying here at the ranch. But I guess the guy's dead in that rollover."

"Earlier, I talked to one of the fire guys who went on the call," I told her. "Besides your description of the car leaving the scene, there was other evidence he did it."

"But why?"

I cupped her chin, made her look at me. "Huck will figure it out."

"Okay."

I dropped my hand. "Now, tell me about this plan of yours."

She blushed prettily. "My plan was for you to find me here."

"Then?"

"That's as far as I got."

I licked my bottom lip. "Want some choices?"

"Sure?" Her eyes dropped to my mouth, and the word came out as a whisper.

"Do you want to come first from my fingers, mouth or dick?"

"That's what's going to happen next?"

I leaned forward, which had her falling onto her back. I set my hand beside her head and leaned over. "You coming, yes. Choose."

Her cheeks flushed, and I couldn't miss the need in her eyes. "Dick. I want you right there with me."

Reaching down, I opened my jeans one handed, pulled my dick free. Fuck, that felt better. I stroked it from root to tip, once, then again. I hissed, my balls aching to be in her.

"Gotta see if you're ready for me first."

I'd always make sure she was right there with me.

Her eyes flared as I kissed my way down her body. She parted her legs for me, and I found her wet. Her folds swollen, her clit poking out hard and eager for attention. I flicked my gaze up her delectable body, met her eyes. She watched me closely then gave me the perfect smile.

Yeah, she was mine. It wasn't going to be simple with Kelsey, but I wouldn't have it any other way.

––––––––

KELSEY

.   .   .

I'D BEEN insane to climb in his window. Insane to strip bare and raid ice cream from his freezer and wait. And wait. But I had to show him I wanted him. Wanted... us. I'd settled myself into the one place I'd fought so hard to be.

The look on his face when he'd come in... priceless. He didn't hate me. He hadn't thrown me out. In fact, now, with his warm breath fanning the inside of my thigh, I believed everything he said. I was it for him.

I was scared shitless, but I wasn't going to let that keep me from being happy.

And when his tongue flicked over my clit, I let my head fall back, my eyes close. When he got his fingers into me, I grabbed his hair. Held on.

He'd never let me fall. He'd always catch me. With that thought in my head and Sawyer's mouth on my pussy, I let go.

Completely.

I came on a breathy cry, the wicked curl of his finger over my g-spot and the ruthless skill of his tongue were my undoing.

He kissed my thigh once, then pushed back, then climbed from the bed. He stripped, letting his clothes join mine on the floor. Shifting onto my knees, I crawled over to him, took a firm grip of his hard cock, and licked the tip like an ice cream cone.

"Kelsey," he practically snarled.

I glanced up at him, met his blue eyes. I felt power here. I made this amazing man lose control. I made him feel good. He found desire and pleasure in my body. In my actions.

It made me realize this truly wasn't one sided. He was giving to me. I wasn't the only one taking. It was an even exchange because we were both in this one hundred percent.

His fingers tangled in my hair and pulled me off him. The crown was slick from my mouth. Red and hard and eager to get in me. "That's not part of the plan," he said, his voice deep and rumbly.

"Neither was what you did. I said dick, not fingers and mouth."

He reached and opened the bedside drawer, pulled out a condom, ripped it open with his teeth and slid it on.

With a hand against my shoulder, he gently pushed me onto my back again, but grabbed my ankles, pulled me to the edge. He didn't let go but lifted my legs, so he held me against his shoulders. "That scream didn't sound like a complaint."

Only then did he push into me.

I groaned. He groaned.

I clenched, he groaned again.

He fucked me then as he stood at the side of the bed, pulling out, thrusting deep. Positioned as I was, I couldn't even lift my hips. I had to take the pounding that he was giving me. I wanted it. Needed it deep. Hard.

His hands released me, and he dropped to his forearms on either side of me, my ankles crossing at his back.

"Sawyer. God, it feels so good," I told him.

"Always, sugar. Always," he said, and I fell apart, coming again.

As he came soon after, dropping onto the bed beside me as we caught our breaths, it would be good. Always. With Sawyer Manning, I'd be happy for now, and I had a feeling happily ever after as well.

———

Ready for more of the Bachelor Auction series? It's time for Huck's story in Back In The Saddle!

I've always wanted her. After all these years, that's never changed.

I thought Sarah O'Banyon had been The One. I'd been f-ing wrong.

I moved on, made something of myself. Became police chief. Even had a beautiful daughter.

When Sarah buys me at the bachelor auction, I'm stunned. It's been *six* years. She wants me for something now. When we end up in my bedroom, I know exactly what. Except I get cuffed to my headboard by the sexy mechanic—and left. Getting free isn't the only thing that's hard.

Turns out she's learned something about my past. A secret which makes her angry. I'm okay with that. It means she still feels *something* for me. I'll change hate to love.

We're going to pick up the pieces of our first love... and our broken hearts because there is no other option. It's Sarah O'Banyon for this cowboy. Always.

A single dad gets a second chance at first love in the next Bachelor Auction book. It's Huck Manning's turn to reignite the flames on his love life... and your ereader.

Read Back In The Saddle!

BONUS CONTENT

Guess what? I've got some bonus content for you! Sign up for my mailing list. There will be special bonus content for some of my books, just for my subscribers. Signing up will let you hear about my next release as soon as it is out, too (and you get a free book...wow!)

As always...thanks for loving my books and the wild ride!

Vanessa

JOIN THE WAGON TRAIN!

If you're on Facebook, please join my closed group, the Wagon Train! Don't miss out on the giveaways and hot cowboys!

https://www.facebook.com/
groups/vanessavalewagontrain/

GET A FREE BOOK!

Join my mailing list to be the first to know of new releases, free books, special prices and other author giveaways.

http://freeromanceread.com

ALSO BY VANESSA VALE

For the most up-to-date listing of my books:

vanessavalebooks.com

All Vanessa Vale titles are available at Apple, Google, Kobo, Barnes & Noble, Amazon and other retailers worldwide.

ABOUT VANESSA VALE

A USA Today bestseller, Vanessa Vale writes tempting romance with unapologetic bad boys who don't just fall in love, they fall hard. Her 75+ books have sold over one million copies. She lives in the American West where she's always finding inspiration for her next story. While she's not as skilled at social media as her kids, she loves to interact with readers.